Praise for Arianna Hart's *Leap of Faith*

"LEAP OF FAITH by the ever creative and always witty Arianna Hart is another exceptional read! Ms. Hart has skillfully crafted a tale filled with action-packed adventure from the very first paragraph, an intense chemistry that leaps off the pages and a plot that is both fast-paced and riveting."

~ *Nadine, Romance Junkies*

"Arianna Hart writes a brilliant story in Leap of Faith... There are twists and turns in Leap of Faith that keep the reader glued to the pages. I could not stop reading it."

~ *Tina, Two Lips Reviews*

"Leap of Faith is high-octane, tension-filled, non-stop action from start to finish. Arianna doesn't let up from the first word to the last. Reading this novel left me breathless and glued to every word. It's an on the edge of your seat, rollercoaster ride..."

~ *Abi, The Romance Studio*

"Leap of Faith was non-stop action from the first page. It is full of danger, suspense, and romance. ...Arianna Hart has become a "Must Read" author when I want a thrilling romantic suspense."

~ *Kathy, Gotta Write Network*

Look for these titles by
Arianna Hart

Now Available:

Snowy Night Seduction
Dark Heat
Spitfire
Surprise
Take Your Medicine
Devil's Playground
A Man for Marley

Leap of Faith

Arianna Hart

A S*mh*in p*bl*shing, Lt*. publication.

Samhain Publishing, Ltd.
577 Mulberry Street, Suite 1520
Macon, GA 31201
www.samhainpublishing.com

Leap of Faith
Copyright © 2009 by Arianna Hart
Print ISBN: 978-1-60504-092-9
Digital ISBN: 1-59998-897-6

Editing by Heidi Moore
Cover by Scott Carpenter

First Samhain Publishing, Ltd. electronic publication: March 2008
First Samhain Publishing, Ltd. print publication: January 2009

Dedication

To Natashya and Charles who liked it first. To Heidi and Crissy who took a chance on it. And to Jenn and Lori who read it so many times and still love me anyway.

As always, this book would never have been written without loads of help from my family. Mom and Dad, thanks for the babysitting time. Paul, thanks for going above and beyond the call of daddy duty. To all of my friends who were ignored as I worked and reworked and obsessed about this book, thank you for not giving up on me. Special thanks to my daughters who waited and waited and waited for me to finish "just one more page".

I'm a very lucky woman, and the people mentioned here are only a small, but very important part of those blessings.

Prologue

The bells above the door jingled, sending her nerves skittering and her body into an instinctive defensive stance. The urge to drop everything and run almost overwhelmed her, but she fought it down. Her shoulder blades twitched, anticipating a bullet. It was never a good idea to have your back to the door—especially a glass one.

Deliberately, she turned around and clutched the pen in her sweaty hand.

No one was gunning for her. Yet.

Releasing a relieved breath, she scribbled Lex's address on the package and got in line behind some old lady mailing a box the size of Texas.

Every little noise shot her heart into her throat and made her already weak knees even shakier. All she had to do was mail this, and hop on the next bus that came down the street. With any luck at all, they wouldn't realize she'd left the compound and she'd have time to make her getaway before they even knew she was gone.

The woman in front of her counted out the exact change from her gaudy, floral purse, and handed it over.

Come on, Grandma, get a move on, she thought as sweat dripped down her back.

The bells rang again, sending her into near cardiac arrest. She was ten seconds from bolting when her turn finally arrived.

"Can I help you?" the pimply kid behind the counter asked.

"Yes. I need this sent to Wethersfield, Connecticut, but I don't have the zip code." Hell, she didn't even know if that was still Lex's address. It wasn't like they exchanged Christmas cards.

Which was why she was sending it to him now. No one would ever think she'd mail him something this important.

She tapped her foot impatiently while the kid looked up the zip code on the computer. Her eyes scanned the street through the windows.

A black Cadillac inched past the strip mall. Crap! It couldn't be them. How had they found her so fast? She tried to hide her face behind a display of boxes, praying they wouldn't spot her in the UPS store.

"Overnight for twenty-two fifty or three to five days by ground for nine ninety-eight?"

"Ground is fine."

The Caddy backed into a parking spot facing the store. This was not good.

"Do you want email confirmation of delivery?" he asked, plodding along like he had all the time in the world.

He probably did. No one was trying to kill him.

"No."

Two guys got out of the car, one the size of a mountain, the other bore a striking resemblance to a scarecrow. Adrenaline surged through her and sweat broke out on her forehead as they headed towards the store.

"Signature confirmation?"

"Sure." Anything to get him moving.

"Just sign here." The kid gave her a pen and she scrawled her name on the bottom and slipped him a ten-dollar bill. He handed her a copy of the receipt and put the box in a bin. "Can I get you anything else?"

"Do you have a bathroom? I'm afraid I'm feeling sick to my stomach." She tried to make her voice waver. It wasn't hard, the fear churning in her gut made her plenty nauseous.

"We don't have a public bathroom."

"Please, I really think I'm going to throw up."

She must have been convincing because he stepped back and pointed. "Down that hall."

She scurried around the counter and headed for the back room. Out the corner of her eye she spotted a delivery truck backing up.

Pulling the door to the tiny bathroom shut behind her, she tore up her receipt and threw it in the toilet. After she flushed it, she opened the door a crack and peeked out. The loading bay was packed with boxes being heaved onto a conveyer belt leading to a truck. She waited another minute until she saw the bin that held her package disappear.

Relief made her head swim. She'd made it just in time. If Grandma had had more packages to mail, she'd have been screwed. She waited until the door to the truck was closed and locked before she slipped out of the bathroom.

A discarded brown baseball cap lay crumpled on the floor. She picked it up and slapped it against her leg before putting it on. The thought of what might inhabit the hat made her shudder, but it was better than getting shot.

As the semi chugged away, she ghosted out the bay door, using the trailer for cover. If she could get to the corner without being seen, she'd blend in with the crowd waiting for the bus.

11

The greasy odor of the diesel engine surrounded her as the truck waited to lumber out of the lot. Nervousness and exhaust fumes had her nausea back with a vengeance. The truck made its turn and she was momentarily exposed.

Her cover was completely blown.

She shot a panicked glance over her shoulder and saw the two goons running for her. The big one reached into his jacket even as he dodged a mother dragging a screaming toddler.

Adrenaline kicked in and she bolted across the street, running for her life.

A screech of brakes sounded right before she felt the impact of car against her flesh. Pain exploded through her body and then mercifully, everything went black.

Chapter One

Fired.

She, Dr. Jane Elizabeth Farmer, had just been canned. Outsourced. Terminated.

And over the phone no less. The little weasel didn't even have the class to fire her in person.

With her cell phone clutched in one hand and her canvas tote bag in the other, she stood stupefied on the front steps of the condo. The late autumn sun shining on her face couldn't warm the coldness that had crept into her heart.

How had her day gone from normal to catastrophic in one three-minute phone call?

Chin up, Jane. This isn't the end of the world, just the end of your radio career. You've handled worse in your life and gone on. You'll handle this too.

The internal pep talk didn't do a heck of a lot to stem the tide of helplessness flooding through her. She'd loved her job as an on-air marriage and relationship therapist. So what if the salary was half of what she'd made in private practice. It wasn't about the money. She wanted to help people, and darn it, her show helped a lot of people.

Not enough people to keep it on the air, apparently.

One hour. She glanced at her watch. She'd give herself one hour to wallow in self-pity and anger, and then she'd put it behind her. Feeling sorry for herself wouldn't solve anything and drowning in it would only be destructive.

Beethoven's Symphony Number Nine beeped loudly, shattering her shell of misery. She'd forgotten she still held her phone in her nerveless hand. When she saw her mother's number displayed on the screen, she had an urge to drop the phone in the azalea bushes.

Guilt kicked in and she answered.

"Jane Elizabeth?"

Who else would be answering the phone? "Hello, Mother. What can I do for you?"

"Oh nothing, dear. I just wanted to say good-bye before Aunt Betty and I head for the airport. Are you sure you don't want to come with us? I bet we could still get you a room."

"No! I mean, I can't take the time off right now." Going on a three-week cruise with her mother and spinster aunt was only slightly less hellish than getting a root canal without Novocain.

"I hate leaving you for so long, but Aunt Betty has wanted to go on this trip for years. And well after that man took her for everything she had, I just don't feel comfortable letting her go alone. Are you sure you'll be all right?"

"I'm thirty-three years old. I think I'll be able to survive."

"Jane Elizabeth! There's no need to be sarcastic. I'm concerned about you."

Oh God. Tension snapped the tendons of her neck as taut as bowstrings. Here it came, the litany of all of her faults and failings wrapped up in a web of her mother's hurt feelings.

"I'm sorry," Jane jumped in, hoping to forestall the drama. "I didn't mean to snap. You're right. I understand that you're concerned about me and I'm sorry for belittling your anxiety."

"Well, it's just I worry." She sounded somewhat mollified. "I'm glad you understand how I feel."

Whew. Eight years of study in the human psyche just paid off in spades.

"I know. I'll be fine here. You and Aunt Betty enjoy yourselves. Take lots of pictures."

A big brown truck rolled up to the curb in front of her condo and a skinny man in a UPS uniform disappeared into the back.

"If you're sure you'll be okay…"

Jane put a hand to one ear to block off the noise of the idling truck and shouted into the phone. "I'll be right as rain, Mother. Have a great time." If it were anyone else on the line, she could use the rumbling of the truck as an excuse to hang up, but not with her mother.

"The cab's here. I need to go now, dear. Take care of yourself, and don't forget to water my plants."

"I won't. Have fun."

A sigh of relief gusted through her as her mother disconnected. Thank God her access to phones would be limited once she was on the cruise ship. Even her mother wouldn't spend eight bucks a minute to nag at her, right?

"Do you live here?"

Jane jumped and almost dropped her phone.

"Yes, I do."

"Sign here, please." The deliveryman handed her an electronic clipboard with a plastic pen attached.

Jane signed on the line and accepted the tiny package he thrust at her. "Thank you," she said to his retreating back. He didn't so much as wave in acknowledgement.

What was this? Jane turned the small box over in her hands and racked her brain to remember if she'd ordered anything on-line recently.

The address on the front of the package caught her eye. Luther D'Angelo, 133 Hopman Way. She lived at 133 Hopman Way, Mr. D'Angelo was at 131. Jane took a step toward the truck to correct the mistake, but even as she raised her hand to get the driver's attention, he chugged out of the complex parking lot.

Okay, no big deal. She'd leave a note for Mr. D'Angelo to pick up his package when he got home. Whenever that was. He was never home, which was just as well.

On the rare occasions he graced the unit with his presence she had to tiptoe in and out of her condo to avoid him and his insolent gaze. When she'd first moved in, he'd cornered her in the foyer they shared. As he introduced himself, he'd stared at her with eyes so hot she'd felt the burn right to her toes. She'd had the irrational urge to cross her arms over her body, as if he'd mentally stripped off her silk sweater and linen pants.

Not only was his behavior inappropriate with a woman he barely knew, it was also insulting. She was a well-educated psychologist with a variety of talents and interests, not some tramp angling to get into his bed.

Even if, by the well-satisfied look of some of the women exiting his condo, he knew exactly what to do in that bed. A warm glow started low in her stomach as she imagined what he must do to put that expression on their faces.

She'd never know.

After their initial meeting, Jane had made it quite clear she wasn't interested in becoming one of the hoards of women who marched through his door. Since then they'd done little more than trade cool, polite greetings and the occasional snipe at one another.

Which was just the way she wanted it.

Even if she caught herself staring at his naked chest when he came back from a jog and imagining what it would feel like to touch all those rippling muscles. He was a playboy all right, and he definitely had the body for it.

Jane shook her head to get rid of the lusty thoughts. Unemployed for five minutes and her normally logical mind had already decided to take a vacation. She tossed the small package into her tote and dug around for a business card to leave on his door. She might as well use them for scrap paper, she wouldn't need them for work anymore.

A dagger of hurt pierced her and her eyes burned with unshed tears. As she printed out a quick note on the back of the card, she fought down the lump in her throat and slipped the note under Mr. D'Angelo's door.

Now what? She had the whole day ahead of her and nothing to do. Go to Nordstrom's and indulge in some shopping therapy?

Maybe not. Now that she was unemployed she'd have to watch her pennies. The trust fund her father had left her would hold her over for a while, but it wouldn't last forever. Part of her wanted to drive to the radio station and give the station manager a piece of her mind, but she forced the urge down.

Her mother would have a stroke if she knew Jane had made a scene. Although, it would feel wonderful to vent her spleen on the spineless jellyfish who didn't have the nerve to fire her in person.

Who was she kidding? She was just as spineless. For all her vengeful thoughts, she knew she wouldn't do it. Good sense said she shouldn't burn her bridges, and of course, Jane Farmer always showed good sense.

Luckily, she still had her volunteer work at the battered women's shelter. Maybe instead of buying things she didn't need or feeling sorry for herself, she'd head over to the shelter and see if any new clients had come in over the weekend. Tomorrow would be soon enough to worry about starting the job search. Right now she wanted to feel useful.

A warm breeze lifted her hair as she crossed to her late-model Saab. The small package tipped out of her tote when she dropped it on the passenger seat. For a brief second, she considered putting it in her condo for safekeeping, but dismissed the idea. It would be secure enough in her car until she got back home.

And if Mr. "I'm-too-sexy" D'Angelo came back before she returned he could just wait for her.

The Saab rumbled to life and she eased out of her parking spot.

A black Cadillac racing around the corner almost clipped her bumper as she pulled out of the complex. Jeez, what's the rush? Driving that fast in a small complex like this was a good way to kill someone. Some people had no regard for the safety of others.

Chapter Two

Flashing red and blue lights lit up the night as Jane pulled into her condo complex. She grabbed her purse and hurried up the sidewalk to where the police officers were gathered. It wasn't until she passed Mrs. Baker's unit that she realized they were congregated in front of her condo.

"Excuse me?" She tapped one of the cops on his shoulder. "Can you tell me what's going on?"

"Do you live here?" he asked.

After spending the day cleaning out a dusty storeroom at the shelter she probably looked like something the cat dragged in. She didn't even want to know how bad her makeup looked or how red and puffy her eyes must be.

"Yes, I'm Dr. Jane Farmer." Anxiety churned in her stomach and her head ached from tension. Her fingers twisted in the strap of her purse.

"Come with me, please." The officer led her past yellow crime-scene tape that blocked off the steps to the entryway of her building.

Her heel caught in a crack in the sidewalk and she stumbled. The officer grabbed her arm and kept her from sprawling face first on the ground.

"Are you okay?"

"Yes. Thank you."

He grunted a response and led her to a middle-aged man wearing the ugliest brown suit she'd ever seen. He was about her height, maybe an inch or two taller than her five feet, seven inches, and had the beginnings of a beer belly.

"Detective Stalanski? Here's Mrs. Farmer."

"Dr. Farmer," Jane corrected automatically.

The detective's eyes squinted at her in appraisal and apparently didn't like what he saw. She lifted her chin and looked the detective in the eye. "Can you tell me what is going on, Detective?"

"I'm sorry to tell you, Dr. Farmer, but you've had a break-in," he said in a gravelly voice of a man who smoked too much.

But it wasn't his voice that made her feel like the wind had been knocked out of her, it was his words.

"I've been robbed?" For the second time that day she felt the world spin and had to force herself to breathe. "What did they take?" Her grandmother's pearls! She almost sagged with relief when she remembered her mother had taken them to wear on the cruise. Thank God. She couldn't replace them, and her mother would never forgive her.

Jane took a step towards the main door but Detective Stalanski stopped her.

"I'll need to get some information from you first while they're dusting for prints. Could you come with me?"

Jane nodded. They crossed the threshold of the common entryway and she gasped. Both her door and Mr. D'Angelo's had been smashed open.

More police officers crowded into the two condos. A skinny man with a Red Sox hat on backwards took pictures as other men and women crawled on the floor and spoke in low tones.

Detective Stalanski tried to move her to the alcove near the mailboxes, but Jane stopped dead when she saw her home. Or what was left of it. Family portraits lay on the floor, frames broken and the glass shattered. Her micro-fiber couch was sliced open and multi-colored throw pillows vomited stuffing.

The refrigerator had been knocked over. Food and milk spilled over her white tile floor. The destruction was amazingly thorough.

"What did they take?" Jane's throat closed up and the words came out in a squeak.

"That's what I want to talk to you about. The thieves didn't take your stereo or TV or any other easily fenced electronics. It appears they were searching for something specific." He flipped open his notebook and slipped a pen out of his pocket. "This isn't your usual smash and grab. A job like this must have taken a long time, especially when you figure they did it to your neighbor too."

"But what could they be searching for? I don't keep money in my house."

"You're a doctor, right?"

"Yes."

"Do you keep any prescription pads or drugs around?"

"I'm a psychologist, not a medical doctor. I can't prescribe medications. And I only have over-the-counter meds in the house." She'd gotten rid of the sleeping pills when she started depending on them every night in order to get to sleep. Being overtired was better than being addicted.

Jane let herself be led away from the carnage. Her brain spun in disbelief. Mr. D'Angelo's house was just as bad. How could someone, why would someone, do that much damage?

Jane answered Detective Stalanski's questions in a daze.

Marital status? Divorced. Any recent fights or altercations? No. Any clients hold grudges? Any jilted boyfriends? No.

"What do you know about your neighbor, Luther D'Angelo?"

"Not much." Other than he had a steady stream of female companions warming his sheets. "He's gone a lot."

"You're telling me this guy has lived across from you for," he glanced at his notebook, "a year and you've never been over to his place?" He raised a shaggy eyebrow at her. "Never shared a drink or maybe caught a movie or something?"

"No." She didn't elaborate. If he thought it was weird she didn't socialize with her neighbor that was his problem.

"Hey, Detective, we're all done in here," a man wearing latex gloves and a blue windbreaker called from her doorway.

"Thanks." Detective Stalanski waved the man off and snapped his notebook closed. "Why don't you take a look around and see if you can find anything missing. If you'd like, I can have one of our female officers wait with you while you pack an overnight bag. You'll want to stay with a friend tonight."

"Yes, of course." She'd stay in a hotel. Most of her friends were colleagues from work, or social friends, but not confidants she'd feel comfortable sharing this unsettling experience with.

"If you call the department they can give you the names of some cleaning services. You'll also need to pick up a copy of the report for your insurance company."

The detective prattled on but Jane didn't hear him over the blood rushing in her ears. Her porcelain cat figurines had been broken into a million pieces. The vases of dried flowers she'd arranged were nothing but dust. Even her plants had been ripped apart.

Every drawer and cabinet in her kitchen was tossed, the

same with her bathroom and bedroom. Jane stepped carefully over broken glass and picked her hairbrush off the floor. All her lotions and hair care products had been dumped out. Even her toothpaste tube was slashed open.

Her closets had been ransacked and her clothes scattered about the room. She had to maneuver around her mattress, which was thrown to the floor, to get to her dresser. A chill shook her as she picked up her underwear. Someone had pawed through her panties and bras.

The thought of putting them on after some sicko fondled them turned her stomach. She knew it was irrational, but she'd rather buy new ones than wear those.

Most of her clothes were covered in broken glass from where the thieves had destroyed her mirror and picture frames. The only items to escape unscathed were a pair of jeans and a T-shirt that were in the dryer. Every suit, sweater, dress and jacket would have to go to the cleaners to make sure all the slivers of glass were removed.

Hot tears trickled down her cheeks. Why would someone do something like this to her?

"Ma'am, if you're ready I'll walk you out." A young, female officer waited for her by the door.

Jane wiped her eyes with her hands and took a quick, shaky breath to get herself back under control. "Thanks."

The officer walked her to the door. Jane waved her off and headed to her car. As she drove out of the parking lot she began to make a list. Tomorrow she'd have to go shopping and replace some of the basic necessities like underwear and—

A hand clamped over her mouth.

"Don't say a word. Just drive."

80C3

Luther "Lex" D'Angelo watched in the rearview mirror as his neighbor's eyes widened. There was a fifty-fifty chance that she'd panic and drive them straight into a tree, but he had to take the risk. If someone had found where he lived, they'd recognize his car too and follow him.

He didn't know what the hell was going on, but he understood when someone was after him. What they'd want with his uptight neighbor, he had no idea.

The emergency recall came to him twenty-four hours ago and he'd come out of deep cover immediately. Changing four planes and two time zones without any sleep or information left him tired, grubby and more than a bit pissed off. He needed a shower, sleep and answers. Not necessarily in that order.

"I'm going to take my hand away, don't scream or you could get us both killed."

The whites of her eyes showed as she widened them even more. Christ, if she got any more panicked she'd freaking hyperventilate. He dropped his hand, but didn't sit back in the seat. No, he wanted to be nice and close in case she decided to turn around and report him to the cops.

"Who are you? What do you want?" she asked, her voice tight.

"What? You don't recognize your own neighbor? I'm crushed." He made eye contact with her in the rearview mirror.

She slammed on the brakes and he almost flew over the seat.

"Jesus, lady! Be careful, you almost killed us both!"

Her hand left the steering wheel and fluttered around her face. "What are you doing in my car, scaring me like that? I almost had a heart attack when you wrapped your hand over my mouth." She turned to look at him. "Do you know your place was broken into? We should go back and talk to the police—"

"No! No police." He loomed over her, trying to intimidate her. "Get moving. Now."

Her hands flitted like startled butterflies.

For a brief second he felt bad about freaking her out, but got over it. They needed to get the hell out of here and if it took him scaring the bejeezus out of her, then so be it.

"Where do you want me to go?"

"Just drive, I'll let you know when to turn."

When they merged into traffic, Lex hauled his exhausted body into the passenger seat and pushed the bags occupying it on the floor. He made sure his gun was still in place under his jacket before leaning back against the seat. It wasn't his usual weapon, but he hadn't had time to get his SIG through customs so he'd had to abandon it.

"Where were you headed?" he asked.

"I was going to find a hotel for the night."

Her eyes kept darting towards him as if waiting for him to attack her. Every time he moved she jumped. Good. If she stayed scared she wouldn't argue as much. Maybe.

Lex didn't know how much longer her fear would keep the broomstick out of her ass, but he'd enjoy it while it lasted. It wouldn't be long before she returned to looking down her snooty nose at him again. Abject terror could only do so much.

"That works for me. I could use some sleep. Make sure you get a room with a big bed. I like to spread out." He pretended to close his eyes and ignored her as she sputtered. His head ached with fatigue and he wasn't sure how much longer he could stay awake.

The car slowed as she drove into a Holiday Inn. He grabbed the bags he'd dumped and got out of the car. She flinched when he wrapped his arm around her shoulders but he ignored it.

"Don't get chatty with the guy at the desk. Do nothing to stand out in his mind, just get a room."

"I don't understand why you're doing this. I'm sure the police want to talk to you about the break-in at your place."

"They probably do, but I don't have time for that now. Just get the damn room and remember what I told you." He took her hand and wrapped it around his back so she could feel the gun under his shirt.

Her face went white and her strangely colored hazel eyes practically bugged out. Little Miss Debutant wasn't expecting that now was she?

Lex chuckled under his breath and nuzzled her ear. When the desk clerk glanced up from his book, he'd see just another couple ready to bed down for the night. Nothing out of the ordinary. That is if he could get Janey here to relax a bit. "Try not to make a scene." He ran his hand down her arm and felt her shiver.

He silently deliberated the intelligence of using her credit card to get a room but decided it was a manageable risk. As far as he knew, Jane was a fine, upstanding citizen who got caught in the cross-fire of his job. No one should be tracking her. Until he got more information from his boss, he had to go on the assumption that whoever trashed their condos was after him and he couldn't use his ID.

God, he hated making assumptions. They always came back to bite him on the ass.

Lex stroked her arm again and tried to act like a guy about to get lucky. Jane stiffened up even more. Instead of looking

26

like a woman about to settle in with her lover, it seemed like she was on her way to her execution.

No wonder she never had any guys at her place. She was probably frigid. Figures. Of all the women in the world he had to get stuck with her. This day couldn't get much worse.

℘℧

Jane's knees shook when gave the desk clerk her credit card. Fear made her palms sweat and she dropped the pen twice before she signed her receipt. She could feel Mr. D'Angelo's hot breath on her neck as he scrutinized every move she made.

She had a sudden urge to ask the clerk for help but then she remembered the gun hiding in the back of Mr. D'Angelo's pants. This made no sense. Why was he hiding from the police? And why did he have a gun? She thought he was some sort of photojournalist. Why would a photographer need to carry a gun?

And would he really use that gun on her?

Yes. There was no doubt in her mind he was a dangerous man. Maybe even a dangerous criminal. He'd already kidnapped her. What would stop him from shooting her in cold blood?

Okay, so he hadn't really kidnapped her. He'd scared her half to death but he didn't make her go anywhere she hadn't wanted to. And he hadn't really hurt her, yet. Sure, he'd wrapped his hand over her mouth, but it wasn't like he'd tried to strangle her or anything.

She dared a quick glance at him over her shoulder as she clutched the room key in her damp hands. He seemed perfectly normal, holding her tote bag while he waited for her to finish her transaction. When she stepped away from the desk, he wrapped his arm around her again and her heart leaped into her throat.

"I wish you would stop doing that. I'm not going to run away," she whispered.

"I'm not taking any chances."

And then the beast held her even closer. When they stepped into the plush elevator he pressed her against the back and nuzzled her neck.

"What are you doing?" She tried to push him away but he held her hands easily in one of his.

"There're surveillance cameras in the elevators. I'm trying to keep them from getting a good look at my face," he murmured against her throat.

A bolt of something hot and tingly shot straight through her from the point where his lips touched her bare skin right down to her toes.

Fear. It had to be terror making her blood pound.

"Stop it! You're squishing me."

When the ding of the elevator signaled a stop, she bolted through the doors and headed for her room. Maybe now he'd quit touching her.

No such luck. He snatched the room key from her hand and pressed her against the door while he lightly kissed her lips.

He smelled of musk and lemony cologne and Jane felt herself go lightheaded.

"Jeez, are you uptight or what?" he whispered against her stiff lips. "Play along, would you? There're cameras in the halls too."

Jane didn't know how to play along with a maniac. First, he accosted her in the car. Then, he practically groped her in the elevator. Now, he was telling her to let him kiss her. She clenched her teeth in frustration.

"Forget it. Let's just get inside." He pushed her behind him before he shoved the keycard into the lock and opened the door.

His eyes scanned the room for a moment before he walked in with his hand on his back—on his gun. A shiver ran down her spine. She knew he was dangerous the first time she laid eyes on him.

"What now?" God, she hated the quiver in her voice.

She sat on the edge of one of the beds. The rust-colored spread matched the heavy curtains over the windows. An uninspired painting of a farm scene hung over the table between the two beds. A small armoire and desk made up the rest of the room.

"Now, we wait." He flopped back onto the other bed and winced before rolling to the side and removing the gun.

Jane averted her gaze as he put the weapon on the table. She didn't like guns or violence. As a psychologist, she believed in talking out problems not shooting at them.

"Mr. D'Angelo—"

"Call me Lex. I think since we're going to be sleeping together you can call me by my first name."

Jane ignored his juvenile comment and the flurry of butterflies in her stomach.

"I don't understand what's going on. Why were you hiding in my car instead of talking to the police about the break-in?" Her brain couldn't assimilate all the disasters that had happened in such a short period of time. Had it only been this afternoon that she'd been fired and felt like it was the end of the world? How much misery could get packed into a few hours?

Thinking about how lousy her day had been reminded her

of the package she'd signed for that morning. She picked up her tote and held out the tiny box.

"With everything that's happened, I completely forgot. This was delivered to my place by mistake. I put a note under your door to tell you I had it but I imagine it got lost when the thieves broke in."

Seeing his large body sprawled out on the mattress made her feel very nervous. He seemed to suck up all the oxygen in the room.

"What's this?" He turned the package in his hands and squinted at the address.

"I don't know. It had my address on the box, but your name. I didn't realize it wasn't for me until after I signed for it, and by that time the UPS man had already left." She tried not to look at him lying on the bed like some giant jungle cat. He was all caged energy and coiled muscles.

It made her more anxious than when he'd clapped his hand over her mouth in the car.

"This could explain a few things." He set it down unopened on the table by the gun.

"Don't you want to see what it is or who it's from?"

"Not particularly. I recognize the handwriting and nothing good can come from it." A frown crossed his face and his dark eyes hardened.

Jane was glad she wasn't the person who'd made him mad. Then she remembered that he might not be thrilled with her for accepting the package. She rubbed her arms as a chill snaked down her back.

Lex swung his legs off the bed and sat up facing her. "Look, I have to make a few phone calls and scrounge up some clothes. I'll be back in an hour. Lock the door behind me and don't let anyone—and I mean anyone—in."

"You're leaving?" He wasn't going to stay with her?

"Just for a little bit. When I find out more about what's going on I'll be back. I'm hoping that if we lie low for a few days I can get things cleared up and you can return to your normal life."

"Really?"

"Probably not," he said, crushing her hopes. "But I'm an optimist. Lock the door behind me."

He stood and tucked the gun into the waistband of his jeans. The package went in the front pocket of his jacket. Jane tried not to stare at his backside as he bent over to tighten his bootlaces, but couldn't seem to tear her eyes away.

Gerard, her ex-husband, never looked like that in a pair of jeans.

Jane averted her eyes when he turned towards her, but his smug little grin told her he'd caught her ogling his rear end. A blush stole into her cheeks.

"Sorry for scaring you earlier. I don't know what's going on yet, but I'll do my best to make sure you don't get hurt." His face held none of its usual mockery or sexual innuendo. He was deadly serious and that bothered her more than she could say.

"Thank you."

He stood so close to her she could feel the heat coming off his body. Jane sucked in a shaky breath and caught the lemony smell of him again. His scent did strange things to her insides, so she moved away from his disturbing presence.

He crossed to the door, opened it cautiously, and looked in both directions before slipping out without a sound.

Jane locked the door behind him. Weariness flooded her body and she sagged against the wall. Now she could curl up in bed and hide under the covers.

Maybe, when she woke up she'd realize this had all been a bad dream.

Right.

Chapter Three

Lex waited until he heard the lock snick into place before he strolled down the hall. At least he knew why his place had been trashed and why they'd hit Jane's too.

Anything that came from Sarah was bad news. That woman could cause problems even while asleep. Now he had to figure out how much trouble she'd stirred up and whether or not he wanted to risk his ass to get her out of it.

He jogged down the eight flights of stairs and slipped out as discreetly as possible. The lobby was nearly empty at this hour.

Once a safe distance away from the hotel, Lex ducked down an alley and whipped out his satellite phone. He punched in the long series of numbers that would connect him to his boss.

Steven "Mac" McLean was the owner of Elite Investigation Services, Inc., a company consisting of former military, cops, private investigators, FBI and CIA employees. Mac hired them out with the skill of a chess master, according to what was needed and who was best suited for the job.

The company had only been in business for five years but already their reputation had grown. Even the government hired them when they didn't have the manpower to throw at a case.

Whether it was protection, recovery or investigation, EIS gave the client one hundred percent. And they were paid well for their results.

Lex had been on assignment in Paris working on a child custody case for a frantic mother when the call came in for him to abort and come home. He'd had enough information to turn it over to the locals by that point, but it still rankled to leave something half done.

"MacLean," Mac barked into the phone.

"What the hell is going on?" Mac's phone would ID him and his location so he didn't waste time with a greeting. "I get the emergency abort call, and come home only to find my place trashed and a package from Sarah waiting for me. I'm hungry, tired and seriously pissed off."

"What package from Sarah?"

"I don't know. That's why I'm asking you."

"When did you get it?"

"Today. Why?"

"Because she's dead."

The words caught Lex by surprise. Not only had Sarah Canterbury been a former CIA agent who worked for EIS, she'd been his former lover. Although things had ended so badly that he never expected to hear from her again, finding out she was dead was still a shock.

"What happened? How?"

"She was hit by a car in Pennsylvania. It appeared to be an accident but witnesses say she was running from somebody."

Lex took the box out of his pocket and looked at the date on the packing slip. Three days ago.

"It's dated the fifth. She must have shipped it right before she got killed. But why me? We weren't exactly close." Anymore.

"I don't know why she sent something to you instead of to the office. Maybe she knew…"

"Knew what?" Warning bells clanged in his head,

something was seriously wrong here.

"Several of our operatives have run into trouble lately."

"What kind of trouble?" The bells rang louder.

"Covers blown, resources gone missing, things like that. Most of the problems have involved work we're doing for the government, but some of the botched missions have been purely EIS jobs. I'd love to blame it on a leak in the government, but I have to prepare for all contingencies, hence the recall."

"Mole," Lex said and swore a blue streak. Mac thought EIS had a freaking mole.

"I don't want to believe it, but I'm running out of explanations."

"Do you have any suspects?"

"A couple, but until I can verify them I want you out of sight. I'm not going to let anyone else die because I don't want to believe we have a traitor."

"I'll lie low for a while but I'm going to need some cash— make that a lot of cash. If our covers are compromised I'm going to have to come up with one of my own and that ain't cheap."

"I'll make a blind drop. After that, do not contact me for any reason. Get away and stay away. I'll contact you once I've caught the spy."

The anger in Mac's voice vibrated through the phone. EIS was more than just his company, it was his passion. The idea that someone would betray him must be tearing him up.

"Roger that. What was Sarah up to? I'll need to watch my back and I don't like the idea of operating blind."

"Don't get involved, Lex."

"I don't plan on it, but I'm not going to walk around with a big target on my head either."

He wanted to open the box and see what Sarah thought

was worth dying for, but he couldn't risk it out here in the open. He'd wait until he was in a secure location and alone. He definitely didn't want the good doctor getting mixed up in any more of this.

Lex heard Mac's sigh loud and clear. "She was working on a fraud case in Stroudsburg, Pennsylvania. Some woman gave her life's savings to one of those TV Evangelists and her son wanted to nail the guy. Claimed he was a con artist preying on old ladies. Sarah agreed to check it out."

"Fraud? That doesn't sound like something worth killing over." His gut told him there was more going on here than a snake-oil salesman conning the blue-haired set.

"And yet, she was. Stay out of it, Lex. I'll make the drop two miles north and a mile east of your current position. Give me an hour to arrange things. I don't want to go through our usual sources on this."

Lex had forgotten his phone had a GPS tracking device hooked into EIS's computers. He'd have to ditch the phone along with his current fake passport and credit cards. Good thing he'd had Jane put the room on her card.

"One hour, got it." That gave him plenty of time to find out what Sarah had sent him.

෴

Jane let the hot water wash away the tension in her neck and shoulders. If she didn't relax she'd end up with a migraine. And wouldn't that just be the icing on the cake?

As much as she wanted to stay in the shower until she wrinkled into a prune, she knew she should get out soon. How long had Lex been gone? The last thing she needed was for him to show up while she was naked.

A tiny thrill zapped her out of nowhere and she remembered his lips on her neck.

Okay, so maybe that wasn't the very last thing she needed.

No, no, no! Get those thoughts right out of your head. Lex D'Angelo was the classic bad boy and she was smart enough to know that any attraction she might be feeling was temporary. How many women had she counseled who repeatedly fell for the exciting bad boy, only to wind up hurt?

Women were drawn to them because they were forbidden fruit. Then they were shocked and surprised when those tempting bad boys treated them like dirt. Jane had never understood the attraction before. Why would someone want a man like that?

But, after spending an hour with Lex, she was beginning to understand the appeal. There was something very sexy about the barely leashed aura of danger surrounding him.

However, she was much too smart to give in to something as fleeting as hormones.

Too smart or too scared?

Jane shut off the water and wished she could shut off her thoughts as well. She wrapped a towel around her chest and sighed. The decision not to take her underwear didn't look quite so smart right now. She'd washed the pair she had worn earlier and hung them on the towel rack to drip dry. Her bra should be okay for another day or so.

She'd have to get some new clothes soon. If she was supposed to "lie low" for a while she couldn't do it with only one pair of underwear. Jane combed her short hair. It had an annoying tendency to curl if she didn't use styling products.

Since her gel was splattered all over her bathroom floor, she had to make do with drying and combing it.

Now, what was she going to sleep in? Her silk pajamas had been covered in glass. She had either the pink cashmere sweater she'd worn all day or the gray UConn T-shirt she planned on wearing tomorrow.

No way would she sleep naked when Lex could come in at any time. She slipped the T-shirt over her head. It came to mid-thigh and hid the fact she wasn't wearing underwear. With her energy flagging by the second, Jane brushed her teeth using the complimentary hotel toothbrush and rubbed some of the complimentary hotel moisturizer on her face.

Her eyes had dark circles under them and her pale skin appeared sickly under the fluorescent lights. Great, she looked like a walking corpse with frizzy hair.

The image saddened her more than it should. Jane turned off the lights. It was only eleven o'clock at night but she was more than ready for bed. The sheets were cool under her bare bottom. She felt exposed and uncomfortable with her near nakedness but was too tired to care.

§∞Ↄ℘

A hand clamped over her mouth for the second time that night, woke Jane out of a rare, deep sleep. Panic shot through her and she struggled to get away.

"Shhh. It's me, Lex, okay?"

Jane nodded her head rapidly. Reality rushed at her when she remembered where she was and with whom.

"Someone found us. I saw a guy flashing your picture at the desk clerk when I came upstairs. We have to get out of here fast."

He threw her jeans at her and turned his back to give her some privacy. Quickly Jane yanked her pants on, flushing at the thought of going without underwear or a bra, but she wasn't about to walk to the bathroom in just a T-shirt to get them.

When she was dressed, he grabbed her purse off the desk and handed it to her while she slipped into her pumps.

"Are those the only shoes you have?" he asked as he dragged her to the door. "Never mind, we don't have time to be picky."

"Wait! My bag is still in there—"

"We have to go." He yanked her out the door.

"But my things—"

"I'll replace them," he growled, the ding of the elevator echoed in the hallway.

Lex bolted for the door marked "stairs" and dragged her along behind him. The clatter of her heels on the concrete steps echoed loudly.

"Lose the shoes," he barked when she stumbled down another flight of stairs.

Jane wanted to protest but he didn't give her the chance. With one steel-muscled arm, he drew her against him and lifted her off her feet. Before she could catch her breath from the feel of his rock-hard body pressed along hers, he'd yanked her shoes off her feet and thrown them out the access door on the next floor.

"Maybe that'll throw them off. Come on."

The concrete was cold and gritty under her bare feet. Her head swam with questions but she didn't have the breath to ask any of them. Who were they running from? Where had he gone anyway?

They didn't stop at the doorway marked Lobby but continued down another flight of stairs. Jane's feet hurt from pounding on concrete and her legs burned from the unaccustomed exercise. Weekly cardio kickboxing classes hadn't prepared her for running down eight floors.

Lex put a finger to his lips and shoved her behind his back as he opened the door. By the smell of oil and the feel of chilly night air, Jane figured they'd ended up in the parking garage.

After a few seconds Lex slipped silently out the door. How could he move in boots without making a sound? Even without shoes she made more noise than he did. Somehow she didn't think that was a skill he practiced as a photojournalist. More questions tumbled around in her head.

Lex slid them around until they were behind the cover of a handicap van. His eyes scanned the area as he held her back. What was he waiting for?

Little clouds of condensation formed in front of her face as she gasped for breath. A shiver shook her frame and she could see that her nipples stood out clearly under the thin T-shirt. Jane tugged her hand out of Lex's grasp so she could wrap her arms over her chest.

"We're going to skirt the edges of the garage until we get to that ramp over there," he whispered in her ear and pointed across the garage. "Keep your head down and do what I do. Understand?"

She nodded mutely. What choice did she have? If she protested he'd probably just drag her along anyway. Jane opened her mouth to ask who they were running from, but he'd already turned away.

Lex crouched down and ran from the cover of the van. He stopped behind the bumper of an old pick-up truck. Jane tried to copy his movements but it was harder than it seemed. Her thighs ached from staying in a partial squat and her feet were going numb from the cold.

They sneaked from one car to the next, staying low and out

of sight. By the time they reached the ramp that led to the parking lot where her car waited, Jane's feet were blocks of ice and her legs protested every step.

Maybe she should have gone to kickboxing class more often.

"We're going to have to make a run for your car. Not enough cover for us to get there easily. You go first. Stay as low as you can. I'll cover you from here. Once you get in the car duck down below the window, and make sure the passenger door is unlocked. I'll be right behind you." He brought the gun out of his waistband and held it with the barrel pointing to the floor "Any questions?"

About a million. Her throat was closed tight with fear and she couldn't get a sound out. She shook her head.

"Good." Lex scanned the area again then gave her a nudge.

Jane took off running, fumbling to get the keys out of her purse as she gasped for breath. Small rocks cut into the tender soles of her feet and pain shot up her legs every time she put a frozen foot on the ground. Her teeth chattered from the combination of cold and fear.

When she was maybe ten yards away from the haven of her car she heard the ding of the elevator in the parking garage. The bell sounded abnormally loud in the quiet night.

The pop of a gun firing was even louder. Jane didn't turn around to see if Lex was behind her. Fear goaded her with sharp spikes and she put on an extra burst of speed to reach her car. Her thumb stabbed the door-unlock button on her key chain and she jumped in.

The engine roared to life and she slid as low as she could go and still see over the steering wheel. Where was Lex? What was she supposed to do now?

Had he been shot? She'd heard more guns firing but she

couldn't tell which direction they'd come from. Her heart pounded like a trapped rabbit and she bit her lip with worry. Should she drive towards where Lex had waited for her?

But that was where the men with guns were. Jane wrestled with her fear and indecision.

Just when she thought she'd have to drive back and get Lex, the passenger door flew open and he dove in.

"Go! Go! Go!"

Jane shifted the car into reverse and screeched backward. Praying no one was behind her, she barely braked before slamming the car into first gear.

"Stay down!" Lex yanked on her arm.

"I can't hit the clutch squished down like this." She got into second gear as her side view mirror exploded. Jane screamed and stomped on the accelerator. She'd figure out some way to hit the clutch staying below the line of fire. Somehow.

₨)₩

Lex laid down some cover fire as Jane sped toward the highway. The smell of cordite in the close confines of the car made his eyes water. His ears throbbed from the report of the gun. The noise was deafening even to someone who was used to it.

Jane must feel like she'd been dropped in the middle of a rock concert. She'd have to deal. There wasn't exactly time to outfit her with ear protection.

He fired a few more shots at the garage, keeping the goons in their position. It'd take them a few minutes to get to their car and hopefully by then, he and Jane would be on their way to New York.

"Take ninety-one south," he ordered as he watched their tail.

The coast was clear, for now. They'd have to switch cars soon though. He'd wait to tell Janey that. She hadn't wanted to leave her stuff in the hotel room, she'd probably go ballistic at the thought of ditching her car.

Now that would be a sight to see. His uptight little neighbor pitching a fit in a ratty T-shirt, jeans and bare feet. Lex didn't think he'd ever seen her in anything but tailored slacks or suits. He knew for damn sure he'd never seen her without underwear.

Until tonight.

When he'd turned around to let her get dressed, he hadn't expected to see her bare butt clearly reflected in the hotel mirror. He knew it was rude, but he couldn't help watching her wiggle into the snug jeans. She had longer legs than he'd noticed before. And that ass of hers was damn near perfect.

It had shaken him up a bit to realize he felt a stirring of attraction for her. When she first moved in he'd thought about tearing up the sheets with her, but one of her haughty looks had killed any interest he might have had.

Something about her cool aloofness had put him off. He was used to women who were full of life, like his sisters. In his mother's house not an emotion went unspoken. At length and at top volume.

Most of the girls he'd dated growing up were Italian girls with softly rounded hips and breasts. They were loud and had tempers equal to his. He enjoyed women who were soft and earthy, not frigid debutants who probably only had sex in the missionary position with the lights off.

Nothing she'd done in the year she'd lived across the hall from him had changed his first impression. Every time he bumped into her, she was frostily polite. The one and only time he'd tried to flirt with her she'd looked at him as if he was a bug that had crawled out from under a rock.

Granted, he'd just walked another woman out to her car after an enjoyable night together, but still. It wasn't like he was propositioning her he was just being friendly.

Whatever. He wasn't going to be flirting with her now. He had bigger problems to deal with. Such as why someone was tracking them down and shooting at them.

EIS did a lot of government work that put their employees in tight situations, but Lex hadn't done any work in that field lately. And it was Jane's picture the goons were flashing in the lobby, not his.

Which meant it had to be something associated with the package Sarah sent. That was the only common denominator. He was going to have to find out what Sarah had been up to that was big enough to get her killed and send armed thugs after him.

He was pretty sure it wasn't a fraud case.

Now, he had to figure out what to do with Janey. He couldn't just leave her on her own with no protection. Whether she wanted it or not. She'd either suck it up and listen to him or risk getting a bullet through her chest.

Maybe that wasn't a fair assessment. She'd reacted pretty damn well for a civilian. She hadn't argued when he'd dragged her out of bed and down eight flight of stairs. He'd seen the questions burning in her eyes but she'd held her tongue.

In his experience, a woman who kept her mouth shut was a minor freaking miracle.

"I think we lost them, but keep moving just in case."

"Where are we going?" she asked, glancing at him out the corner of her eye.

He knew her silence was too good to last.

"Pennsylvania. Take six-ninety-one to eighty-four west. Wake me up when we get to Brewster, New York." He released the seat lever and lay back as far as he could go.

Maybe she'd keep quiet if she thought he was sleeping?

Not a chance.

"I have a few questions I'd like answered, please."

"Like what? I can't tell you everything. That's for your own safety so don't pester me about it." He peered at her through half-closed eyes.

She looked offended by his words and he chuckled to himself. Needling her was so damn easy. And amusing too.

It was the only thing easy or amusing about this whole damn mess.

"First of all, who are you, really? I know you're not a photojournalist."

"Oh? Why do you say that?" He used the photojournalist cover with the management company of the condo complex so they wouldn't get suspicious as to why he was gone so much.

"I don't believe photographers carry guns with them." She fiddled with the controls and the heat bumped up another notch.

He was already sweating from running across the parking lot, but she was still shivering.

He decided to level with her—to a point. "You're right, I'm not a photojournalist. Although I've known several who routinely carried weapons." In the jungles of South America but he didn't tell her that. "I work for a company called Elite Investigation Services. We find kidnapped children and take care of...other things."

"That's why someone is shooting at you? Because of a

kidnapping or because of one of those 'other things'?" She stared at him incredulously.

"No. This doesn't have anything to do with one of my cases."

"Then I have to assume it has something to do with the package that was delivered today?"

He pointed his index finger and thumb at her like an imaginary gun. "Bingo."

"But why would they look in my apartment? I have nothing to do with you or your business."

"The box was sent to your address. You probably signed for it, right?" He waited for her nod of assent. "A teenager with a good computer can hack into the delivery records to find out where the package went and who signed for it. If they knew where Sarah sent it from and through which company, they probably were at your place ten minutes after the box arrived."

"So if I hadn't signed for it, they wouldn't have destroyed my home?"

Lex felt a stab of sympathy for her. This was so far out of her depth she must be drowning in shock. "I'm afraid so."

She was quiet for a moment. After a minute she asked, "Who's Sarah?"

"An associate of mine."

"What was in the box?"

"Information that pertains to another case. That's all I can say."

Sarah had sent him a jump drive wrapped in about ten layers of bubble wrap. She hadn't wanted anything to happen to the data on the keychain-sized storage device.

Lex had gone to a cyber café to check out the drive while he waited for Mac to drop off some cash. It contained names, dates and dollar amounts that were well into the millions. It'd take someone much more knowledgeable about accounting to figure out what it all meant, which is why he'd left it at the drop point for Mac. Lex didn't want to risk losing something that small with vital information on it.

Vital enough for Sarah to die for.

"So what are we going to do now?" Jane asked just as he was drifting off.

"We're not doing anything. I'll do some digging and you'll lie low for a while. There are some complications within my company right now. Until they're resolved you'll need to stay out of sight."

"For how long?"

"Not long. But until it's safe you'll have to fly under radar. Think of it as a vacation."

He hadn't thought much about what to do with the good doctor. After he'd gotten the money from Mac he'd headed back to the hotel for a few hours of shuteye only to spot a guy flashing Jane's picture to the desk clerk. He'd hightailed it up to the room, dragged her out of bed and ran.

Now he didn't know where the hell to put her where she'd be safe. The goons who had gotten Sarah were after Jane now and she didn't have a tenth of the resources Sarah'd had.

Crap.

If he tried to stash Jane in a hotel somewhere she'd be dead in an hour. With the possibility of a mole at EIS, he didn't dare put her in one of the safe houses.

He was stuck with her.

Chapter Four

Jane followed Lex's directions, driving in silence. The only other vehicles on the road were tractor-trailers that rumbled by, rattling the car as they passed. Two o'clock in the morning and she was wide-awake. For once her insomnia was useful.

Except it gave her too much time to think. Gee, that was a surprise. Gerard had always teased that her mind never shut off. Later in their marriage he'd complained about it, told her she didn't know how to loosen up.

Wouldn't he be surprised to see her now, driving barefoot, without underwear and braless with a man like Luther D'Angelo sleeping next to her? The fact that gun-toting lunatics were trying to kill her because of a mysterious package would've sent him into complete shock. Things like that just didn't happen to people like them. Intellectuals, who could trace their roots to the Mayflower, didn't run from criminals—or with them for that matter.

Could Lex be a criminal? She wasn't sure how much of his story she believed. If he really did work for an agency that rescued kidnapped children, then why hadn't he wanted to talk to the police? He had a lot of explaining to do. And she'd demand some answers as soon as he woke up.

She stole another look at him. In sleep, his features softened some, but not much. Without his intense eyes to distract her, his nose seemed to dominate his face. His full lips were slightly parted to allow his deep, even breathing.

A shiver that had nothing to do with her cold body shook her frame and she forced her attention back onto the road. Almost against her will her eyes crept back to look at his face under the passing streetlights.

He had olive-toned skin with thick, dark stubble covering his jaw. A thin scar graced his cheekbone. Funny, she hadn't noticed that when he'd held her so close earlier.

A rush of heat flooded her body as she remembered him nuzzling her in the elevator. It had all been for show, but it had still dazed her. Was she so desperate for affection that any male attention aroused her?

No. It'd been a long time since she'd been held in a man's arms, that's all. And she'd never been held by someone so, well, totally male before.

Even asleep he seemed to take up more space than his body accounted for. He wasn't that much taller than she was, but he filled the car to capacity. Jane wasn't a small woman by any means, but he made her feel tiny and helpless.

And he was sound asleep. When he was awake it was even worse. It felt like his life force sucked the energy out of the room and left her wilted and lifeless.

Darn it, that wasn't right. She shouldn't feel weak just because she didn't run around playing spy and carrying a gun. She was an intelligent woman with multiple degrees and it was time she stood up for herself.

And she would...when the time was right.

Who was she kidding? She was such a coward. His brusqueness intimidated her. Facing confrontation wasn't one of her strong points on a good day. Voluntarily entering into a conflict with a man who carried a weapon like she carried lipstick was way out of her comfort zone.

Still, she couldn't just keep doing whatever he told her without thinking for herself. Up to this point she'd followed his directions like a docile puppy.

Okay, so in the beginning he'd scared her into submission. She'd had to do what he said then. But she could have slipped out of the hotel room after he'd left. She didn't have to stay where he put her. He was asleep now. She could take the next exit and go...

Where? Where would she go? She couldn't go back to her condo. Obviously she couldn't go back to the hotel with the gun-toting maniacs. And there was no way she'd lead them to her mother's house. So where did that leave her?

Doing exactly what she was doing.

How pathetic. The only direction she had in her life came from running away from men with guns, with a man she didn't trust as far as she could throw him.

How had she let her life get so out of control?

"Take the next exit for US two-oh-nine," he said, rattling a sheet of directions he'd taken out of his pocket.

Jane jumped at the sound of his voice. He'd been snoring a second ago. How did he wake up instantly and figure out where they were and what exit they needed to take, just like that?

She had her blinker on and was taking the exit before she even realized she'd automatically followed his directions. All right, enough was enough. Time she took some control over this situation instead of blindly following his every command.

As soon as they were off the highway, Jane pulled the car into the lot of an abandoned gas station.

"Do you want me to drive for a while?"

"No. I want you to tell me where we're going and what

exactly we're going to do when we get there."

"I told you, we're going to Pennsylvania. Stroudsburg, to be exact. When we get there I'll figure out what we'll do next."

"I don't want to go to stay in Pennsylvania with you. Why can't I take you to Stroudsburg and go on my way?" Not that she had a way to go on, but he didn't know that.

"Did you forget about the men with guns behind us?"

"They're after you, not me. As sorry as I am that someone might be trying to kill you, what it boils down to is that's your job, not mine."

"Honey, they were flashing your picture to the desk clerk, not mine. They're after you as much as they're after me."

"That's ridiculous. I have nothing to do with this at all. Why should they be after me?"

"Because you signed for the box. These guys don't care if you're a doctor or a thief all they care about is tying up loose ends."

"But surely if I explained I had no idea what was in the box, that it was only a mistake they'd—"

"Wake up, Pollyanna! This isn't Sunnybrook Farm. This is the real world with real criminals shooting real guns."

"It was Rebecca of Sunnybrook Farm, not Pollyanna, and I know there are awful people in the world. I'm not naïve."

"Sweetheart, you have no idea what's out there. And it's my job to make sure you never do."

"Be that as it may, I'm not moving this car another inch without more information. If indeed these men are after me, I deserve to know why."

"It isn't safe."

Jane's stomach roiled in fear but she didn't let up.

"You've said they'll kill me regardless of what I know, so why don't you just tell me?" She clenched her hands in her lap so he couldn't see them trembling.

"Fine. Have it your way, but when you can't sleep at night, don't blame me."

Too late, mister. She already couldn't sleep at night and it had nothing to do with him.

He stared at her again with those piercing, dark eyes. In the dim light they seemed more black than brown and it took every ounce of nerve she had to meet his glare. Finally, he ran a hand over his face and to the back of his neck.

"Sarah mailed me a jump drive. Do you know what they are?"

"They're those little things you can put on your key chain. You can plug them into just about any computer and store a bunch of information on them." When she was in private practice she'd stored her case notes on one so she could review them at home if need be.

"Right. This one had a bunch of information on it with dates, names and dollar amounts. Big dollar amounts."

"Where did she get it?"

"I don't know. She'd been working a case up in the Poconos. Some guy wanted EIS to investigate James Robert Beaupree, a TV preacher. The client claimed his mother had been conned out of all her money by Beaupree."

Jane's heart dropped to her toes. She knew far too well how devastating it was to watch a family member surrender her life savings to a slick-talking con man. It had taken months for her Aunt Betty to recover after she'd been scammed. It wasn't just the financial devastation either. The embarrassment and humiliation of being taken for a fool was almost harder for her to survive than the loss of her life's savings.

"My boss said Sarah took the job and reported there was something besides a shell game going on there. She was going to try to get into the inner circle and dig a little deeper before she wrapped it up. That was the last he heard from her until he got the call to identify her body."

Jane let out an involuntary gasp. The woman who sent the box was killed for the information on it. That meant whoever was behind this wouldn't hesitate to kill her either.

"Mac, that's my boss, thinks someone within EIS blew her cover."

"You mean someone you know could be responsible for her death?"

"No, I think the Tooth Fairy is responsible."

Jane ignored his sarcasm. She'd heard worse in her practice.

"I'm sorry. I shouldn't have snapped at you." Again the hand went over the face and scratched at the stubble. "I haven't slept much in the last thirty-six hours and the idea of a traitor at EIS pisses me off."

"You're upset, that's understandable." She automatically slipped into therapist mode. It wasn't unusual for patients to lash out at the therapist when facing traumatic events. Knowing someone you trusted was responsible for your friend's death could definitely be considered traumatic.

"Hell yeah, I'm upset but that doesn't mean I have to be a bastard to you. Why don't you let me drive for a while and you can get some sleep?"

"I'm fine. I got some sleep at the hotel. Can you tell me what we're going to do when we get to Stroudsburg?"

"I don't know yet. But I think we're going to have to ditch your car."

"My car?" She loved her Saab. Sure, it was a late model, but it still ran like a trooper.

"Look, if these assholes have your address and picture, they probably have your plate number and the make and model of your car too. If we don't lose it somewhere, it'll lead them right to us."

"But I got this when I graduated from college. It was a present from my father." She felt like crying. First, her job had been taken away, then her home, now he was trying to take away her car, her only link with her father.

"I'll make sure you get a new one after all this is over. Maybe not a Saab, but at least a new car."

"I don't want a new car. I want this one."

"More than you want to live? Is a hunk of metal worth your life?"

Tears of frustration burned behind her eyes. When he put it like that, no it wasn't worth her life. But darn it, it was her car. She clutched the steering wheel in a white-knuckled grip as if she could hold onto it by sheer dint of will.

"We don't have to do it right now, but soon. If you want, I can take care of it for you."

"If it's at all possible, do you think I could get it back when this…situation is resolved?"

"I can't make any promises, but I'll try my best." He laid a hand on her cheek. Little jolts of heat pulsed from his fingertips through her body.

"Okay."

"Now can we get going?" He dropped his hand and settled back into the seat.

She felt chilled at the loss of contact and shivered.

"Are you still cold? Jesus, I'm dying over here." He shut off the heater.

"That's because you didn't run over frozen ground barefoot in nothing but a thin T-shirt and jeans." She pushed the heat back up.

"It wasn't that cold out, just a little nippy."

"Maybe since you were properly dressed it didn't feel cold, but to me it did."

"Lady, I walk around in shorts until December. Trust me, that was nothing."

She looked at him out the corner of her eye. He practically exuded heat and energy while she felt like an ice cube. "I'm always cold," she said, more to herself than to him.

"That's because you have no meat on your bones. If you spent a week with my mom you'd put on a few pounds and be as warm as I am."

He smiled at her and his teeth gleamed in the glare of the streetlight. Jane's stomach flipped again.

"I go to kickboxing twice a week to make sure I don't put on any extra pounds, thanks all the same."

"I'll never understand women. I've lived with the species my entire life and it's still a mystery to me why they starve themselves just so they can look like some bony little boy."

Jane stiffened and lifted her chin up a notch. She knew she wasn't well-endowed but that didn't mean she looked like a boy.

"Maybe we do it because we're constantly judged by our appearances?"

"Don't give me that line of garbage. Men like breasts. It's hard wired into our DNA. There's no escaping genetics, you know."

"Believe me, I know." Jane clenched her teeth to keep from snarling at him.

Gerard had apparently found her lacking in that aspect of her genetic make up, because he'd left her for his secretary and her 38-DD, DNA.

It still rankled her that he'd been willing to throw away their five-year relationship and their successful counseling practice for a pair of mammary glands.

Oh, he'd fought her on the divorce, saying it was an aberration and they could work through it. He'd even gone so far as telling her getting a divorce would ruin their reputation in professional circles.

When that hadn't worked he'd blamed the whole event on her, saying if she had been more open, more accepting of his needs as a man he wouldn't have looked elsewhere. That had been the death knell as far as she was concerned. After five years of boring, unfulfilling sex he was the one complaining about his needs being met? It had been too much for her pride to take.

Somehow she didn't think Lex would leave any partner of his unfulfilled after lovemaking.

Chapter Five

"Turn in there. We need to get some supplies before we go any further." Lex pointed to the nearly deserted parking lot of a Wal-Mart. Thank God this one was open twenty-four hours.

He'd been looking at the map and a germ of an idea had begun to form. An idea he was almost positive Jane wasn't going to like. Too bad. He didn't much care whether she liked it or not.

She didn't say anything, for once, just obediently parked the car close to the front of the store. Her eyes had dark circles under them and her face looked pinched with fatigue, but she hadn't voiced a complaint. If he'd made one of his sisters drive all night while he slept, his ears would be ringing for a week.

He didn't get Jane. Not one little bit. But that didn't stop him from sneaking glances at her while pretending to sleep. Although she wasn't lushly sensual like most of the women in his past, she had a classic beauty that intrigued him.

Just because she wasn't his type didn't mean he couldn't appreciate her attributes. The way her nipples pebbled up under her thin T-shirt had him imagining things to do with those attributes that would probably shock her right out of her cotton panties.

Oh yeah, she wasn't wearing any panties.

His body tightened instantly, hardening at the thought of her shucking off her tight jeans to reveal her naked ass for a more thorough investigation.

Down boy.

What the hell was wrong with him? This was his stick-in-the-mud neighbor he was fantasizing about. Get real. If he came on to her she'd stick her nose up in the air and stalk off like the Queen of freaking England.

"What are we doing here?"

"I told you I'd replace the things you had to leave at the hotel. Here we are. Do you have any other shoes? I don't think you can go in barefoot even here in the back end of nowhere."

"I have a pair of flip flops that I keep for when I get a pedicure. I think they're in the back seat."

She wore a shell-shocked expression that tugged at his heart, but he pushed it away. They didn't have time for her to fall apart. She'd just have to suck it up until he could figure out what was going on and who was after them.

Jane unbuckled her seatbelt and reached into the back seat for her shoes. The scent of soap and woman drifted over him, charging his libido like a lightning bolt. Her breasts pressed against the thin shirt and his mouth watered.

It must be jet lag. That had to be what was making him think of Jane as some tempting morsel instead of the iceberg she was. It would pass.

Damn it, it had better pass. He couldn't afford to get distracted by his hormones.

"I cannot believe I'm going out in public like this," Jane muttered ruefully.

"What? Wearing jeans, a T-shirt and flip-flops? That's the uniform for half the United States' population."

"Not for me. I've never gone out of the house without any—ah—in this condition before."

Without any underwear.

She couldn't say it but he understood all the same. The picture of her curvy little butt shimmying into her jeans flashed through his memory, making him almost lightheaded as his blood went south in a rush.

"Trust me, no one will even notice. It's six o'clock in the morning. No one's going to pay any attention to you at all." Except for him. Good Lord did he notice. "Come on. Let's get moving. We've got a lot to do and not much time to do it in."

Ⅎℳ

Jane tried to hunch over so no one could tell she wasn't wearing a bra. Although, Lex was right, no one even looked twice at them as they pushed their cart through the aisles.

She'd picked up a couple changes of clothes and toiletry items as well as a pair of flannel pajamas and some sneakers. Hopefully, it would be enough to last them until she could go home and hit Nordstroms.

Her mother would drop dead if she saw Jane shopping in Wal-Mart, wearing flip-flops and jiggling freely under a ratty T-shirt. Good thing she was more resilient than her mother.

Lex had gone off with the cart while she'd been searching for a new bra. Her face had flamed as he offered his opinions on which bra would be the best. She'd shot him a quelling glare, but something had made her grab the raspberry demi-bra instead of the plain white one she'd been looking at.

And the lacy underwear she'd chosen had nothing to do with him at all. They were just on sale and it made sense to buy the frivolous three pack instead of the cotton grandmother underwear that was the same price.

By the time she found Lex, the cart was filled to the brim and he was headed for the check out line.

"Did you pick up a jacket? You might want to grab something to keep you warm. The nights can get pretty cool in the mountains."

"Mountains? What are we going to be doing in the mountains?"

Lex swore a blue streak and pulled her behind a magazine rack as headlights flashed across the store windows. "I'll explain later. Stay out of sight. As soon as this stuff is rung up, take as many bags as you can and prepare to run."

Adrenaline shot through her, making her knees weak and heart pound. Even though Lex appeared to wait patiently as the cashier checked out their items while carrying on a conversation with the clerk in the next lane, Jane could see the barely leashed energy churning in him. His eyes scanned the parking lot continually and he practically bounced on the balls of his feet.

As soon as the last item was rung up, Lex handed over a wad of cash before stuffing Jane's arms with blue bags. What the heck had he bought anyway? She hadn't paid attention but it was a lot more than some clothes and a toothbrush.

He pocketed the change then gathered the rest of their purchases. Jane headed for the automatic doors but he stopped her in her tracks.

"Hold on. I need to check this out before we walk blindly into a trap."

The car that had pulled into the lot while they were in line was a black Cadillac, just like the one that had almost run her down yesterday.

And it was parked in front of her Saab.

Lex swore again.

"Come on, there has to be a back door."

Jane's arms ached with the weight of the bags she carried, but she was too scared to complain. Lex held even more than she did and he managed to move along just fine.

"Would you slow down? I'm going to fall if you keep pushing me like that."

"Then move faster."

She practically ran through the shoe department to a door marked "Employees Only."

"We can't go in here. It says employees only."

"So arrest me. We need to get out of here without our buddies in the Caddy seeing us. It won't be long before they get sick of waiting and come into the store, if they haven't already."

Lex led her to a garage door that was partially open. Gas fumes and cigarette smoke lingered in the air.

"Wait here while I make sure they don't have someone covering the back door. If you hear shots, run like hell and scream your head off. They won't try anything with this many witnesses."

Gunshots? Again?

Dropping his pile of purchases, Lex pressed her behind a forklift and slipped out the door. A shiver danced down her spine and she clutched the packages closer to her chest.

What on earth was happening to her?

Her heart raced and sweat dripped down her face as she imagined a million catastrophes. What if he left her here? What if he got shot? Worse, what if she got shot? What if right this very second someone was coming to get her?

A whimper tried to claw its way out of her throat but she bit it back. How long had he been gone? She strained her ears to pick up any little noise but all she heard was the rushing of traffic in the distance.

Her knees almost buckled when a car pulled up to the docking bay. Lex burst out of the front seat and charged toward her.

"Move it, Janey. I knocked one of the guys out but he could come to any second. The other one is in the store right now."

Her head still spinning from fear, Jane ran as fast as she could in flip-flops over the dew-covered pavement. Lex had already thrown his bundles in the back seat and motioned for her to hurry up.

"C'mon! Get in."

A pebble jabbed the arch of her foot through the thin rubber but she ignored it as she practically fell into the front seat of the huge car.

She wasn't even buckled when Lex put the car in gear and crept out of the driveway.

"Keep down." He pushed her head next to his thigh, crushing the bags she still held to her chest.

"Are they after us?"

"Not yet. When we didn't come out the front door, the big guy went into the store. I waited until he was in before I got you. If luck is on our side for once he won't find his missing partner right away and that'll buy us some time."

"So can I sit up?"

"Not yet. They'll be looking for a blonde so I want to keep your head out of sight as long as possible."

"This is vastly uncomfortable." The seatbelt cut into her stomach and her face was pressed just inches from his jean-clad leg. She could smell the musky odor of sweat and man and it did strange things to her insides.

"Not as uncomfortable as a bullet in the head."

Good point. She wiggled around to try to find a better position. Her face brushed against his thigh and he let out a groan.

"Could you please keep still?"

"I'm sorry. I'm doing the best I can. I've never had to lie across the front seat of a car before."

"What a shock."

"What's that supposed to mean?" She tried to lift her head up to get a better look at him but he pushed her head back down.

"Forget it. You wouldn't understand."

He was laughing at her. She could hear it in his voice. "Just because I don't run from gun-wielding lunatics on a regular basis is no reason to make fun of me, you brute. I'm doing the best I can under the circumstances."

"I'm not making fun of you. Really."

"It sure sounds like you are."

A gust of air ruffled her hair as he sighed. "When you were a teenager, did you fool around in your boyfriend's car?"

"Of course not!" Her mother would have killed her. Ladies didn't "fool around" at all, but most especially not in a car. Not that Jane wouldn't have been willing to try it at least once if she'd had the opportunity. Unfortunately, her dates in high school were limited to chaperoned events orchestrated by her mother.

"I didn't think so."

"What does my youthful experience," or lack thereof, "have to do with being squashed against the seat?"

"Lady, you don't want to go there. Trust me."

"Right. Like I'd trust you about anything."

"Whaddya mean by that crack?"

"You have to admit, you're not the most upstanding of citizens."

"What're you talking about? I was a freaking FBI agent!"

"You run away from the police, you carry a gun, and you have a penchant for, ah, playing the field." Her face flamed in embarrassment, but she didn't back down. If he was going to mock her for her lack of experience, she could comment on his plethora of it.

"My what?"

"The revolving door on your bedroom."

"You're crazy. I'm not a player."

"Oh pul-lease. If you had any more women parading through your condo you'd have to install one of those 'take a number' machines like at the deli. You are most definitely a player." Whatever that was.

"Not that it's any of your business, but I've had relationships with all the women who've 'paraded' through my room. Jesus, it's not even like there's been that many. I'm not home enough to be a player."

"It's none of my business how you choose to live your life." Oh Lord, could they please just drop this subject? She should have kept her mouth shut. This was only slightly humiliating.

"You're right. It's not." He tapped his hand on his thigh.

Jane couldn't help but stare at his long fingers just inches from her nose. He had a strong hand, very masculine with a smattering of dark hair sprinkled across the knuckles. It would look perfectly natural holding a beer can or a hammer. She couldn't picture Lex drinking from a wine glass or using a

64

delicate fish fork with those broad, callused hands.

An image of his fingers cupping her breasts, his darkness against her lightness, flashed through her brain, singeing every synapses along the way. He wouldn't be a gentle lover. No, he'd be hard and demanding and probably very thorough.

Her breath hitched as her heart rate shot through the roof. Suddenly she felt far too warm. Sweat trickled down the back of her neck and between her breasts.

"I am not a player."

"Whatever you say."

"Don't try that reverse psychology crap on me. Just because I don't live like a monk doesn't mean I use women. They know the deal going in. I'm not around enough for a permanent relationship. That's not what they're looking for either. Just a mutually satisfying experience between consenting adults."

"Of course." Very satisfying, from what she could tell.

"Why am I explaining myself to you?"

"I have no idea."

Lex swore softly and Jane hid a smile. The conversation was completely inappropriate, but he was no longer picking on her for not making out in a car as a teen. It was nice to actually win a battle with him for once.

"You can sit up now."

"Thank you." Jane's head spun slightly as she righted herself. "Would it be possible to stop for something to eat soon?" Her stomach growled as if to emphasize her point.

He grunted but didn't answer her. His forehead was scrunched up in thought.

She didn't want to ask again, but if she didn't eat soon her blood sugar would drop to her toes and she'd probably pass out. Her stomach rumbled even louder.

"I hear you, I hear you. We've got to ditch the car before it gets reported stolen and the cops start looking for it. I don't want to leave it just anywhere because I don't want a trail pointing right to us. I've got to find a place to stash you and the gear safely while I get us new wheels."

"You stole this car?" And she was in it. That made her an accessory to the crime. She'd be arrested. Her name would be in the paper and everyone would see that she'd been involved in a grand theft auto. Her reputation would be shot.

"No, I asked politely if I could borrow it. Of course I stole it, how do you think I got it?"

"That's illegal!"

"Mac will handle it if we get caught. Which I don't plan on happening. Ah, perfect."

Jane turned to see what was so perfect and spied a big silver trailer. A neon sign reading "Mom's Diner" blinked overhead. Several tractor-trailers were already parked in front of it. Lex slipped in between two semis, the big rigs completely dwarfed their stolen sedan.

He used the bottom of his T-shirt to wipe off the steering wheel and the door. "We'll eat here and figure out what to do next."

That was fine with her. She'd never eaten at a truck stop before but she was too hungry to care if she got food poisoning. She grabbed her purse from the floor of the car and heaved the car door open. Copying his actions, she wiped the handle and shut the door with her hip.

Lex waited for her, bouncing on his toes as she tried to finger comb her hair and straighten out her shirt. A smile tugged at the corners of his lips when her stomach voiced its complaints—loudly.

"Come on, let's get a table before you pass out from hunger. You're tiny enough as it is." He held her arm and walked her up the metal steps to the door.

"If you tell me I'm as skinny as a boy again, I'm going to smack you," Jane warned.

Lex let out a loud laugh and she shot him a death-glare.

"I never said you look like a boy. And even if I did, there's no mistaking you for one in those jeans." His eyes grew hot as his gaze roamed over her hips and legs.

Although tingles bubbled in her veins from his gaze, she said, "You called me a skinny little boy in the car."

"No I didn't. I said I'd never understand why women starved themselves to look like skinny little boys. I never said you were one."

"Well that's how it sounded."

"Then I apologize. Trust me, I never once thought you appeared anything less than a lady in all the time I've known you. At least until today." He gave her a mock bow and held the door open for her.

Mom's Diner didn't have a diverse menu, but if you liked grease, it was the place to be. Jane rearranged her silverware into the correct placement, scrubbing the fork and spoon with a napkin she yanked from the dispenser in the booth.

"Here's the plan. After we eat, I'm going to hide you and the stuff somewhere then ditch the car."

"What about my car?"

"We'll get that back later. Don't worry about it."

"That's easy for you to say. It's not your car."

"I'll take care of it. Jeez, you need to relax, take some of that starch out of your spine."

Her back immediately stiffened and her chin shot up, as

she prepared for battle. "Just because I'm looking out for myself doesn't mean I need to relax. Maybe I'd be more relaxed if you weren't constantly pushing me around without even telling me what's going on."

Lex shot her a scorching glare but didn't say anything as the waitress came over with coffee and poured two steaming mugs of the liquid heaven.

"What can I getcha?" She tugged a pencil and an order pad out of her apron.

"I'll have the hungry man special, eggs over easy, bacon, a bagel with butter, and a glass of orange juice. Oh, and could you make sure the hash browns are well done?"

Jane couldn't believe he could possibly finish all of that and still walk afterward. There wasn't an ounce of fat on him. There was no way he ate like that regularly.

She opened her mouth to order a grapefruit and a side of dry rye toast, but that's not what came out. "I'll have a tall stack of pancakes with bacon and an orange juice."

"Sure thing, sugar."

Where had that come from? She hadn't had pancakes since her grandmother died—her mother sure as heck hadn't made them. Jane took a sip of coffee to cover her shock over her mouth betraying her, again.

Good God, this was the best coffee she'd ever tasted.

"Damn, if you ever looked at a guy like you're looking at that coffee, he'd be in heaven."

"A man has never given me as much pleasure as this coffee."

Where had that come from? Heat crawled up her neck.

"Then you've obviously been with the wrong men." Lex's eyes danced with amusement as he picked up his mug.

The laughter stopped when got a taste of the brew. "Holy crap, you're right. This is incredible. I guess the old urban myth is right. Truckers always know the best places to eat."

Jane tried not to notice the way his throat moved when he swallowed the coffee. For some mysterious reason she wanted to press her lips against that strong column and lick her way up to his mouth.

Another flush of heat washed over her. She'd had next to no sleep, been on the run from gun-toting lunatics, been an accessory to a crime and now she was fantasizing about kissing her playboy neighbor. She needed to get her head examined.

Physician, heal thyself.

Right.

Chapter Six

Who knew the great outdoors could be so unnerving? Jane sat with her back against an enormous oak tree, surrounded by blue bags that looked as completely out of place on the leaf-strewn ground as she did. Lex had left her here over an hour ago and she'd barely moved from the spot.

Her bladder was ready to burst, causing her to regret that last cup of coffee. She had no idea where they were other than somewhere in the Poconos. If Lex had to "stash" her somewhere while he did his thing—whatever that was—why couldn't it have been somewhere with a comfortable couch and a bathroom?

How much longer was he going to be gone anyway? She glanced at her watch yet again. Oh goodie, one more minute had passed. She really had to pee.

Jane had no choice. She was going to have to relieve herself behind a convenient bush. Her mother would be horrified, but it was better than wetting her pants.

Of course, if her mother knew she'd gone shopping braless and in flip-flops, she'd probably have a stroke anyway so what was one more transgression?

Good lord, what was wrong with her? Her house had been broken into. She was on the run from God only knew who, and she was worried about her mother's reaction if she found out

Jane peed in the woods? Talk about having her priorities skewed.

Jane straightened her shoulders and pushed herself to her feet. She was made of sterner stuff, no matter how she'd acted so far. Whining never solved anything. There was no excuse for sniveling about the calamity her life had become.

It was time to take control of the situation. And the first step was to relieve her over-full bladder.

Brushing leaf mold and whatever else from her bottom, Jane went in search of an appropriate tree. It wasn't like there was anyone around to see her bare behind, but she didn't want to pee up hill either.

The air felt chilly on her naked backside as she dropped her jeans. She couldn't keep the blush from heating her face even though she was all alone.

Ridiculous. Lex would laugh his fool head off if he realized how embarrassed she was. He didn't have any problem walking around half-naked, that was for sure. There had been more than one occasion where she'd met him in the foyer they shared getting his mail in nothing more than a tiny pair of cut-off shorts or cotton boxers. She'd had to avert her gaze from the acres of bronzed skin he shamelessly flaunted without an iota of embarrassment.

What a pair they made. She was mortified to pee in the woods when no one was within five miles of her, and Lex could walk around practically naked in the middle of a city. Were there ever two more mismatched people to get stuck together?

Jane drip-dried to the best of her ability and carefully stepped around the puddle she'd made. There, she was a real nature girl now. She'd urinated in the woods. Let's hear it for girl power.

Oh boy, she needed to get a life if relieving a bodily function made her feel like Wonder Woman.

A rustle in the trees off to her left made her jump out of her skin. She froze in the act of buttoning her jeans and listened for another sound.

Something was out there. Something bigger than the chipmunks and squirrels that had been racing overhead. Whatever it was, it was strong enough to push aside the saplings dotting the forest floor.

Her heart beat so hard she thought it was going to pop out of her chest. Every breath she took sounded abnormally loud and harsh in her ears. Sweat dripped into her eyes and she blinked rapidly to ease the sting as the creature moved closer and closer. Branches crashed as whatever it was made its way through the underbrush.

Blood rushed through her veins. A sneeze tickled her nose, but she held it back.

The dappled sunlight played peek-a-boo around the heavy foliage overhead, distorting her view. There was definitely something big moving but she couldn't see what. Snuffling snorts echoed against the tree trunks.

Oh God, could it be a boar? Were there even wild pigs in Pennsylvania? What would a branch do against fierce tusks? With her luck, she'd be gored and bleed to death before Lex got back.

A whimper squeaked out of her throat.

With a flurry of movement, the animal broke cover and leapt through the brush. A doe and her fawn stared back at her, before running off with a flick of their white bob-tails.

Jane remained frozen for another second before the relief washed over her, making her muscles weak. Laughter burbled as her knees collapsed and she landed in a heap on the ground.

Oh yeah, she was the brave white hunter, ready to take on a terrified deer and her baby. Tears leaked from Jane's eyes while she gasped for air. Every time she tried to get herself under control, she'd remember the look on the doe's gentle face and started laughing again.

Maybe all the cataclysmic events finally broke down her psyche or perhaps it was just her body's way of dealing with extreme stress. For whatever reason, it took her forever to calm down.

"What's so damn funny? I could hear you laughing a mile away. Why don't you just rent a billboard to announce where you are?" Lex stepped into her clearing making her jump again, which brought on a new spate of hysteria.

"It's just a reaction. You missed me bravely fighting off two dangerous foes. Or should I say does?" She actually snorted at her own joke.

"Uh, Jane? Are you okay?"

"No. I'm far from okay, but I'm managing. What took you so long?" She did her best to pull herself together. Strangely, she felt more relaxed than she had since yesterday, before she got the call telling her not to go into work.

"I had to get a car through legitimate channels which took a while, and I needed to do some recon and get some supplies."

"More supplies? We're going to need a Sherpa to carry all the stuff you've bought."

"I like to be prepared."

"Prepared for what? The Armageddon? How long are we going to be gone anyway?"

"I don't know. That's why I want to be prepared. So tell me, Janey, have you ever been camping?"

"You can't be serious. My idea of roughing it is a bad

Holiday Inn."

His face was dead serious. He wasn't joking.

"Then it's time to expand your horizons. We can't risk staying in one place for any length of time so camping it is. Grab those bags and let's get back to the car. I want to organize our supplies to make them easier to carry."

℘)Ƈ

Lex bit back a grin as he glanced at Jane strapped into the backpack he'd filled with their clothes and food. She'd almost tipped over when he'd put it on her. His backpack was heavier by far, but she obviously didn't think so. If looks could kill, he'd be split in two.

Her faded jeans clung to her hips and for some reason he couldn't stop looking at her. She'd changed out of her flip-flops and put on her new sneakers, and presumably her new bra and underwear too. He remembered how she looked without them though, and it was killing him.

He'd lived next to her for a year and they'd barely exchanged a pleasant word, and now he was sweating thinking about her going commando. Damn, he needed to get laid badly if he was becoming obsessed with her.

How long had it been anyway? Contrary to her belief, he didn't sleep around like some rutting dog. When he was on an assignment he never made time for female companionship. Sex was a distraction he couldn't afford on the job.

He'd gone from one job immediately to the next, now that he thought about it. Christ, no wonder he was so hot for his uptight neighbor, it had been close to six months since he'd scratched his itch.

And it didn't look like he was going to end that drought any time soon. His body might respond to Jane's, but that didn't mean he had to act on it. He liked his relationships to be nice and simple. And it didn't take his superior detecting skills to recognize that nothing about Dr. Jane Farmer would ever be simple.

His groin tightened uncomfortably in his jeans, mocking him.

"Keep moving. We don't have a lot of daylight and I want to set up camp before the sun goes down." He'd set a pace that would be sure to exhaust the good doctor. Maybe if she was bone tired she wouldn't realize there was only one tent and a small one at that.

More blood rushed south as he pictured Jane's delicate face being caressed by firelight. His body tensed as his imagination spread her naked body out on the sleeping bag he'd purchased. He could almost smell her subtle feminine fragrance as he kissed his way over her stomach.

Stop it right there, buddy. He had to focus on the mission, not trying to get his neighbor naked. Wouldn't that just prove to her that he was the playboy she'd accused him of being?

Not that he cared what she thought. Just because she lived like a nun didn't mean he had to. There was nothing wrong with the way he lived his life.

"How much farther?"

It was the first thing she'd said to him since they started their trek hours ago. He hadn't bothered to stop for lunch because they'd had such a big breakfast and he really wanted to get to the spot he'd marked on the map before nightfall.

"Not too much. We'll set up camp on top of that rise over there. You can make it that far, can't you?"

"Of course." Her cheeks were red and her blonde hair stuck to her sweaty head in springy curls.

She was going to be sore tomorrow, but at least she wasn't screaming complaints at him. If he'd forced his sisters to make the hike, carrying a good thirty pounds of supplies, they'd have nagged him every step of the way. His sisters weren't known to suffer in silence.

Jane wasn't the only one who'd be sore tomorrow. His calves burned as they pushed through the underbrush up the hill. Granted, his pack was significantly heavier than Jane's, but he was used to physical labor, she wasn't.

By the end of this mess she would be.

Chapter Seven

She should have known better than to wear new Keds without socks. The blisters on her feet had burst hours ago and now the skin around her ankle looked like raw meat. So far, she'd managed to keep Lex from noticing her damaged feet but she had no idea how she was going to walk another step tomorrow.

This great outdoors business left a lot to be desired. What she wouldn't give for a hot shower and a massage right now.

The clatter of poles falling, followed by Lex swearing a blue streak distracted Jane from her misery. Lex had taken his shirt off while they set up camp and the firelight painted his olive skin a deep bronze.

His muscles bunched and rolled as he tried to erect the tent and Jane's mouth watered. A drop of sweat rolled down his back and she wanted to follow its path with her tongue.

A tight coil of need spiraled low in her belly, making her body tingle in places long neglected. Her breasts felt heavy and swollen as she thought about pressing against Lex's lightly furred chest. Was there any give in that steely frame? Would he crush her?

"Hey, Doc, think you could lend me a hand here?"

"S—sure." She had to clear her throat to get rid of the huskiness.

Shake if off, Jane. This is no time to forget he's a playboy.

Just because he looked like a bronzed god didn't mean she could forget her common sense.

Watching Lex's arms bunch and roll as he fought to bend the tent pole, she thought she might have another clue about the bad boy syndrome and what made them so irresistible.

Stop that!

Hello? She was a psychologist for heaven's sake. There was a rational explanation for why she felt this increased level of attraction to a man totally unsuited for her. In extremely dangerous situations such as these, it was normal for her to want to bond with the man in charge. Add in the fact that he was attractive and dangerous in his own right, well, that just upped the ante.

When all of this was over, the insane desire she felt for him would be over too. And although he might not mind having a fling, she wasn't emotionally equipped to have casual sex.

Therefore, she would ignore the tingles and focus on getting her life back without compromising her integrity.

"Could you help some time this century?"

"I'm coming, keep your pants on." She hobbled over to the patch of dirt he'd swept clean of rocks.

The internal pep talk did nothing to quell the lust churning through her body as she got closer to him and saw those muscles glistening with sweat. There was something so elementally male about him that called to her female side.

"Hold this loop while I bend the pole to fit in it."

"Yes, sir."

"Do you want to sleep in a tent tonight or out in the open?" His annoyed glare singed her skin.

"I'm holding the loop already."

With a few more swears and a lot of straining, Lex managed to get the tent set up. The nearness of all that naked skin did nothing to help her remember why she had to keep her distance and not allow herself to make idiotic choices.

"What the hell happened to your feet?" Lex shouted, snapping her out of her internal struggle for common sense.

"I just have some blisters from walking so far in new shoes."

"Some blisters? Your feet look like steak tartar. And you're walking around barefoot? I thought you were smart."

Before she could protest—because of course she would have protested—he scooped her up and carried her toward the fire.

"This isn't necessary. I'm fine."

"Right, I can tell. If those get infected you could be in serious trouble. Why didn't you tell me?"

"Would you have stopped?" It was almost impossible to have an intelligent conversation with him when her heart beat like a trapped rabbit's. She stared at the stubble along his chin and wondered if it would feel rough against her thighs.

Good heavens. Get those thoughts out of your head.

"Probably not, but we could have put some bandages on before they got this bad. Stay here while I heat up some water to wash them."

He set her gently on an ancient tree stump while he put a pan of water on the fire. "I bought a first aid kit. It should have something for your feet. Good thing we're staying here tomorrow."

"I thought you said we couldn't stay in any one place for too long?"

"We can't, but chances are no one is going to be searching

the forest for us. We'll be able to spend a few days here before we move on. Hopefully by then your feet will have healed some. Let me see them."

Jane winced with embarrassment as he took her mangled foot in his large hands and began cleaning it. Burning pain shot up her aching legs as he rubbed ointment over her tender skin.

"Hang on, almost done." He finished wrapping her foot and laid it on his thigh before running his hand up her lower leg.

Her head fell back as he massaged some of the tightness out of her calves.

"I'll give you one, maybe two hours to stop that," she sighed.

"I figured your legs would hurt after the hike. You held up a lot better than I gave you credit for."

"I do kickboxing twice a week."

"I remember you saying that. It shows. I think you did great."

"Really?" It was humiliating how much his words meant to her.

"Really. Now just sit here while I make dinner."

"First aid and room service, what more could I ask for?" Was she actually flirting with him?

"Don't go there, babe." His deep brown gaze trapped her and wouldn't let go.

She felt he could see through her and read the scandalous thoughts running through her brain. He maintained eye contact for a second longer before turning away, breaking the sensual spell that'd held her enthralled.

Her brain shrieked warnings but her body didn't listen. Her libido had emerged from its hibernation hungry as a newly woken bear.

ℰↄↃ☙

Lex cleaned up the supper dishes with the last of the water in the gallon jug. He had two more in case they didn't find clean water nearby, but he wouldn't be sorry to have less weight for the next trek.

Although, how they were getting to the next camp site he'd picked out on the map was anybody's guess. Jane couldn't hike ten yards with those blisters covering her feet. He still couldn't figure out why she hadn't said something earlier. She was tougher than he'd suspected.

Had he pegged her all wrong? She'd always seemed so snooty. He'd loved freaking her out by getting his mail in his underwear. The horrified expression on her face had made him laugh every time.

When he'd been putting the tent up she hadn't looked horrified, she'd looked...hungry. And he wasn't laughing now.

Oh no, he was feeling far from amused. Jane was inside the tent washing down with the baby wipes he'd bought, preparing for bed. He'd carried her there himself, almost groaning from the feel of her breasts pressing against his chest.

At least tonight she'd be bundled up in a sweat suit. Hopefully that would keep her hardened nipples from poking up and tempting him.

"Okay, I'm decent," she called from the tiny tent.

"I'm almost done. I'll be there in a minute."

In the six by six foot space that they had to share tonight. With her.

She hadn't balked about their sleeping arrangements nearly as much as he'd expected. Maybe she was just too tired to argue? That could be it. She'd almost fallen asleep in her beans twice before he carried her to bed.

His groin tightened at the image that phrase brought to mind. He'd brought Jane to his bed. Their bed. They were all alone out here. Maybe she'd get scared and want to cuddle up next to him. After all, it wasn't like they were strangers. They'd lived across from one another for a year.

During which time they'd done little more than throw insults back and forth.

Right. She thought he was a player. There was no way Miss Uptight Dr. Farmer was going to crawl into his sleeping bag.

Unless she wanted a no-strings-attached fling.

Nah, that wasn't her style. And even if it was, he wasn't a player and he wasn't going to be used as one. He could control his over-active libido and keep his sleeping bag—and his pants—zipped.

"Do you need anything else out here before I crawl all the way in?"

"No, I'm fine. Thank you."

She was coolly polite again. Good. That would keep him from remembering the way her breasts had jiggled under her shirt.

Sure it would.

It was a challenge to snake his way into the sleeping bag without smacking Jane, but he did it with a minimum of swearing. Once he was settled and had his gun in easy reach, he clicked off the flashlight.

The darkness was all-consuming. He'd tamped down the fire before turning in so there wasn't even the flicker of flames against the tent wall to break up the night.

"Wow." Jane's voice sounded much too close to him.

"Yeah. You don't realize how much light pollution we're used to until you come to a place like this."

"No wonder our ancestors worshipped fire."

"I never thought of that before. I just enjoyed looking at the stars."

He heard her rustling around and realized she'd turned onto her side to face him. "Did you do much camping as a kid?"

"Are you kidding me? I grew up in Brooklyn. The only campfires we ever saw were the ones in barrels with street people clustered around them."

"Then how do you know so much about the wilderness? You got us here and set up camp like a pro."

"Wilderness training. The first time I had to find my way out of the woods by myself, it took me two days and I almost died of dehydration. I made sure I learned a lot about following a compass and a map after that."

"Good thing."

"I'll show you how to read the map and use the compass tomorrow in case we get split up."

He heard her sudden intake of breath and felt her tense up. Without thinking, he reached out and touched her face to calm her down. The feel of her soft skin under his fingers shot bolts of heat to his groin. He was thankful for the darkness that hid his reaction.

"It's not that I'm scared or anything." Her voice was barely a whisper.

"I think you'd be an idiot not to be scared. You've been yanked from your comfortable life and dropped in the middle of an unknown forest. I don't plan on leaving your side for long, but if something should happen you need to be able to find your way to safety."

"What are you going to do? About all this I mean? How are you going to find out who's after us?"

"Don't worry about it. That's my job. I'll think of something." Hopefully.

Lex dropped his hand and tucked it back inside the sleeping bag where it belonged. His fingertips still tingled from the contact so he rubbed them against his jeans to get rid of it. He needed to think of a plan, not wonder how much softer the rest of her body might feel.

୫)୯୫

A heavy weight crushing her stomach and a rock digging into her hip woke Jane from the sleep of the dead. It took her a few minutes to orient herself as to where she was and whose arm was thrown over her.

Lex.

Lex's arm held her tightly to him, pressing her backside into his groin through their clothes and sleeping bags. There was nothing improper about it, but her cheeks filled with heat just the same.

Moving only an inch or so at a time, Jane managed to slide out from under his hand without waking him. He snorted once and rolled onto his back, flinging his arm over his head. She froze and waited to see if he'd wake up, but he continued to snore softly.

His beard had grown thicker overnight and made him look scruffy. But scruffy in a good way. A very sexy, good way.

Stop ogling him and find a bathroom before he wakes up.

Her good sense had terrible timing. Jane patted the puffy sleeping bag until she found her flip-flops and slipped them on over her bandaged feet.

The ground was wet with dew and the leaves twinkled in the morning sunlight. The forest looked like it had been coated with fairy dust overnight and the sight took her breath away.

Birds called to one another from their perches and squirrels jumped from branch to branch. The lack of mechanical noises was bizarre. No cars zoomed by on the highway, no telephones rang or TVs blared. She felt like the only person in the world.

Jane took a deep breath of the cool, morning air and held it for a count of ten. Her body ached. More than ached, it throbbed. Her thighs felt like someone had taken a meat tenderizer to them and her shoulders screamed every time she lifted her arms.

Thank God they weren't going anywhere today. She didn't think she could handle another workout like that just yet.

Her sigh misted the air in front of her as she went off in search of a "little girl's bush". She was getting to be an old hand at this. Great. She could add "can pee in the woods" to her resume.

Ugh. Her resume. With everything that had happened in the last two days, she'd forgotten about getting fired. Losing her job was the least of her worries right now though, so she gladly pushed the depressing thought away.

"Denial isn't just a river in Egypt," she murmured as she shuffled back to camp.

The fire had died down to tiny embers. It occurred to her that Lex must have gotten up to tend the fire at some point during the night, but she hadn't heard him.

Closing her eyes, she tried to recall how he'd lit the fire in the first place. He'd built a little tepee with twigs and bark. Once that got going, he added more wood to it.

Well, she already had a coal there, so if she threw some twigs and bark on it, logically, it should start up again.

In mere minutes, she had a cheery fire burning and snapping. She looked at the blaze and felt prouder than when she'd made the Dean's List. Maybe she wasn't such a baby after all.

By the time Lex rolled out of the tent she had hot water boiling for the instant coffee she'd found in the backpack. They'd have to share a mug as the tin mess kit he had didn't come with a second cup, but she didn't care. As long as she had caffeine she was happy.

"You're up early. How'd you sleep?"

"Surprisingly well, all things considered. I have coffee if you'd like some."

"You're a goddess. I'll be right back."

Jane watched him pad off to the woods almost silently in his untied boots. How'd he do that? He should be clumping along like an elephant instead of gliding like a panther. Must be something else they taught him in wilderness school.

It was kind of nice to have Lex be pleasant to her. Last night when he'd realized her fear, his touch had been gentle and soothing. And the way he'd taken care of her feet had been deliciously tender.

There was more to Lex D'Angelo than just a handsome face and a hard body. Although that body was nothing to sneeze at. He stretched his arms overhead as he came into camp, as though working out some lingering soreness. His T-shirt rode up and Jane got a glimpse of six-pack abs and the sexy curve of his pelvis.

A shiver ran down her spine and she had to raise the mug to her lips to make sure she wasn't drooling.

"I hope dry toast is okay with you. I didn't want to risk trying to carry eggs." Lex broke some twigs off a long branch and speared a slice of bread with it.

"As long as I have coffee I don't care what we have to eat."

"Let's see if you're still saying that after you've eaten hot dogs and beans for a week straight."

"A week? You think it'll take that long?"

"Probably longer. Someone wants the jump drive Sarah mailed me. Wants it enough to kill for it. This isn't TV, we're not going to figure it out in an hour."

"But how? How are we going to find out who is after the jump drive, what they're doing wrong and why they want to kill us over it?"

"*We're* not going to do anything. I am."

"If you're not going to involve me, why can't you leave me somewhere else? Certainly your agency has safe houses or whatnot."

"Sure they do, but I can't trust any of them right now. I don't know for sure that there's a mole at EIS, but I trust Mac. And if he says our covers aren't safe then I believe him."

"So you're just going to leave me alone out here in the wilderness while you run around playing secret agent man?"

"Pretty much. We won't be safe until Mac gives the all clear and I find out why Sarah was killed. Which means I'll be investigating her last case while you keep yourself out of sight and out of trouble."

Jane bit back a smart remark. She might feel like a superhero because she survived the trek up the hill and peed in the woods, but she was a psychologist, not an FBI agent. Or whatever he was now.

He was right. She couldn't be much help in finding out who

was after them.

"So what's on the agenda? I'd like to give my feet another day to heal, although they feel much better this morning," she said after they finished their dry toast.

"I'm going to do some recon. I have a plan but I need more information before I can put it into action. While I'm gone, you can color your hair."

"Excuse me?"

"I bought some boxes of hair dye. Pick which one you want to use."

"I'm not dying my hair." She paid good money to get her blonde highlights and she wasn't ruining them.

"Yes you are. They're showing your picture all over the place so you have to change your appearance. I'm going to do it, too, don't worry."

"Easy for you to say. You have about two inches of hair. It'll grow out in a month. I haven't been a brunette since I was sixteen."

"Whatever. Just pick one and be done with it. I have to do a recon. I'll be back in a few hours. Don't go anywhere."

Then he planted a kiss on her lips and disappeared.

Chapter Eight

The compound Lex spied through his binoculars looked more like a military fort than a religious retreat. A twelve-foot fence enclosed a cinderblock building. Black-clad guards patrolled the perimeter and security cameras scanned the grounds.

If it wasn't for the neon cross and sign that read The Great Hope Ministry, he'd think he was scoping out a prison instead of a church. There was a lot more going on here than some con man stealing retirement money from little old ladies.

Not that there weren't plenty of them filing into the building. A shuttle bus brought a dozen or more blue-haired passengers every half hour. They shuffled into the building chattering happily to one another. None of them seemed the least bit disturbed by the fence and guards.

Damn it, he needed to get down there and into that building. What was James Robert Beaupree protecting?

What type of vice made the amounts of money he'd seen on the jump drive? Drugs, gambling, weapons dealing, white slavery? The location was too far out in the sticks for a high-profit gambling ring. That left arms, slavery or drugs.

He'd keep his options open, but Lex was putting his money on drugs. They weren't near enough to any major shipping ports for easy transportation of weapons or human cargo. The gambling angle didn't feel right, but it was a possibility. Hell, anything was possible, that's why he was doing a recon. God, he hated going in blind.

Lex crept away from his observation point and eased closer to the building. He kept his binoculars trained on the people coming and going from the ministry building. If he could catch one of the guards unaware, maybe he could snag the uniform and sneak in for a better look.

They were well-trained, that was for sure. Someone with a brain had organized the guard rotations. They mostly kept within sight of one another or the cameras.

Crap. He'd have to wait until dark before he could try anything. Which would mean leaving Jane alone in the forest at night. That would go over like a fart in church.

He'd never had to worry about his partner before while on a mission. And hopefully he'd never have to again. Trying to solve the mystery of Sarah's death and keep Jane safe was a pain in the ass.

This whole situation sucked. He had no backup, no resources and his "partner" was a freaking socialite. Might as well pick one of the women getting off the shuttle bus to be his partner instead of Jane. At least then he could get some intel about what the inside of the building looked like.

The kernel of an idea began to sprout in his brain. What if he used Jane to get some inside information? He trained the field glasses on the shuttle bus again. With the exception of a few tottering old codgers, every person getting off that bus was a woman.

Most of them were AARP candidates, but there were some younger women mixed in. If he could disguise Jane well enough, she could mix in with the others and get in and out without anyone the wiser.

Wait a minute. What the hell was he thinking? He couldn't send Jane on a mission. She wouldn't know the first thing about gathering intelligence. It was too dangerous to send an innocent inside.

He'd have to figure out a way to sneak in himself. There had to be at least one or two young guys joining the mission. It couldn't be all females. He settled himself in to wait.

After two hours his butt had gone numb, his eyes were blurry and he was chilled straight to the bone. He was also frustrated as hell.

Not a single guy under the age of seventy had gotten off that bus. In fact, the only young men he'd seen were the guards. He was going to have to take one out and try to impersonate a guard at night. There was no other way for him to get inside.

But Jane could.

He swore in English, then Italian, then some gutter Spanish before he felt better. She was a freaking civilian. What the hell did she know about undercover ops? She'd blow her cover in ten seconds flat.

Or would she?

How hard would it be for her to blend in with the other housewives and attend a service? She wouldn't be trying to investigate, just get the layout of the place. It couldn't be that dangerous if all these old ladies came and went freely.

Crap. He'd have to put it to Jane and see what she thought.

God help him.

෨෬

Mud. Her hair was the color of mud. Jean Claude would

never forgive her. Without a mirror she couldn't get the overall impression of her new "do" but from what she could see in the bottom of the pan, she looked as plain as a sparrow.

Wonderful. She didn't have a hair dryer so she couldn't blow her hair out straight. It curled wildly all around her face. She was sure she must look like she'd stuck her finger in a light socket.

The jeans she'd picked up at Wal-Mart slid so low on her hips she had to wear the baggy sweatshirt to keep her belly from showing. She didn't have a speck of makeup on, and her hair was a dirt-colored mop. At least she didn't have to go out in public like this.

Where the heck was Lex? It was getting dark and he hadn't come back yet. She didn't know whether to start dinner—such as it was—without him or wait.

How would he react to her with her hair like this? Not that she cared what he thought about her looks, but she was vain enough to want to appear attractive.

Right.

Like he would even look twice at her if she wore a silk dress and had her hair professionally done. She'd seen the type of women he was interested in. They all had big boobs and curvy hips and oozed sexuality.

He thought she was as skinny as a boy.

Not that it mattered. It wasn't like she wanted his interest or anything. Okay, so she wouldn't mind it too much if he at least acknowledged that she was a female.

Get real, Jane.

After her disastrous marriage to Gerard, she knew better than to lie to herself. She told her patients they had to face reality if they wanted to grow. It was about time she listened to herself.

Lex was a devastatingly sexy man. She'd known that from the first time she'd seen him. He'd scared her with his blatant masculinity so she'd responded by turning her nose up at him. She'd pretended that his lifestyle and behavior were repugnant to her because that was better than facing the fact she was afraid he'd find her sexually inadequate.

Now that they were thrown into this chaotic situation, and in constant contact with each other, she couldn't fool herself any longer. She knew her interest in him had more to do with his bulging muscles than his moral character, but that didn't seem to matter.

Her head cautioned her that even if she did manage to attract his attention as something more than a burden, as soon as this was over he'd drop her like a hot rock. After all, any attraction between them could very well be due to the circumstances. Life or death situations amplified emotions, especially ones that led to procreation of the species.

After this mess was resolved and the adrenaline wore off, he'd go back to his playboy ways. Even if he wasn't the player she'd accused him of being, he definitely didn't have lasting relationships that she'd been able to see.

So what? Her libido prodded.

So what? The thought of casual sex scared her down to her toes. Or worse, the thought of rejection after casual sex frightened her. What if she wasn't any good at it?

Oh my, had all these fears been lying in wait for her all this time? Her divorce had been final over two years ago. She'd thought she'd dealt with the humiliation of Gerard's betrayal and her feelings of inadequacy. But had she?

Obviously not because she hadn't had a physical relationship since the divorce.

Maybe it was about time to change that?

Heavens. She had to think this through before he got back and she did something impulsive like jump him. What if, hypothetically, she did sleep with him? If she went into this with her eyes open and had no expectations? Could she use it as a way to face her fears and just enjoy herself instead of trying to make a relationship out of it?

Yesyesyesyes!

Her lips tingled as she remembered the brief kiss he'd given her before he left. It probably hadn't even registered to him that he'd done it. More than likely it was a habit to kiss the woman he'd slept with goodbye. But it had thrown her for a loop.

And if that didn't tell her she needed to have more physical relationships with men, what would? If a scant brushing of lips had her head in a tailspin, what would sex do to her?

She didn't know, but boy did she want to find out.

Jane fanned her hand in front of her face, feeling awfully warm all of a sudden.

Pulling off her sweatshirt, Jane tried to think logically about what her hormones were urging her to do. If a patient came to her and confessed fears of intimacy to her, what would Dr. Jane Farmer recommend?

Certainly not a fling. But she would suggest to her patient that in order to get past her fears, she'd have to face them.

And what better way to face them with someone as hot as Lex?

Gosh, she wished her libido would be quiet. How was she supposed to think this through with her body going up in flames at the thought of touching all that bronze skin? Her breasts felt heavy and swollen. Oh boy, Lex thought she was a prude, if he could see what she was thinking he'd be shocked down to his toes.

What could she do about all the need swimming through her system? Was she brave enough to approach Lex? Sure, their relationship wasn't as adversarial as it had been in the past, but he still wasn't looking at her as a potential bedmate.

Could she change that?

Could she seduce Lex and therefore overcome her insecurity about her sexual prowess? Was that even fair? Wasn't that using him?

Hello! This was Lex she was talking about. He was a walking advertisement for casual sex. But that didn't mean it was right to use him. Of course, if she explained the situation and was perfectly honest, that wouldn't be deceiving him now, would it?

The thought sent conflicting bursts of fear and excitement through her.

Could she really do it? Was she strong enough to lay her pride out on the line like that? Nervousness made her knees weak just thinking about sex with Lex. She couldn't even stand up to a startled doe without almost wetting her pants. What made her think she'd be able to seduce Lex without chickening out?

"Oh good, you dyed your hair."

"For heaven's sake! Could you announce your arrival before you sneak up on me? You frightened me half to death." Her heart was indeed racing, but it had more to do with her thoughts than his sudden appearance at their camp.

"Sorry, I thought you saw me come in."

"No, I was...lost in thought. Did you find out everything you needed to?"

He snorted and shook his head as he dug out another box

Arianna Hart

of hair coloring. "Not even close. I found the target but I don't have the right equipment to get in."

"What type of equipment do you need?"

"Another X-chromosome."

"Huh?" Jane couldn't seem to stop looking at his hands as he tossed the box back and forth. How would those fingers feel on her? In her?

"Just about every person going into the ministry was a female. If I can't take out one of the guards, I'm not going to be able to get inside. And if I can't get inside, I'll never be able to find out what was so important about those numbers Sarah sent me."

He ripped open the box with more force than necessary and took out the bottle of colorant. After snapping off the top, he raised it over his head as if to dump it in one shot.

"Wait! What are you doing?"

"Dying my hair blond. What does it look like?"

"You have black hair. If you try to color your whole head it'll come out orange."

"What do you suggest? I need to change my appearance too."

"Hold on. Let me think." Her mind spun furiously. He couldn't ruin that beautiful jet-black hair by turning it orange. "Won't you stick out more if you're walking around with hair the color of Bobo the Clown?"

"I know the problems. I'm not hearing any solutions though."

"Did that box come with a cap?" She had an idea that just might work.

"You mean this thing?" He held up a plastic baggy.

"That'll work. Do you have one of those Swiss pocket knives

96

with a million attachments?"

Lex dug around in his pocket and tossed her the bulky gadget. There, it had tweezers, just what she needed.

"Perfect. Now sit down here on this log while I give you a highlight."

"Excuse me? Didn't you just say I couldn't dye my hair?"

"This is a highlight, it's different. I'm going to pull little sections of hair through the cap and dye only those sections. You'll look like Ricky Martin."

"I don't know about that. I want to blend in, not stand out."

Like a guy who looked like him could ever blend in with the crowd? "Don't be a baby. You want to disguise yourself, here you go." She pushed him down and tied the cap over his head before he could protest any more.

A chill breeze rattled the branches and brushed across the strip of exposed skin between her shirt and her pants. Jane thought about putting the sweatshirt back on, but it was so baggy it would get in her way and end up covered in bleach. She tugged her shirt lower to cover her tummy.

Lex let out a groan and she peered at him questioningly.

"If you want me to sit still, don't yank your shirt down like that."

Jane glanced down and saw the scooped neck of her shirt had dropped low enough to expose the edges of her raspberry colored bra and a great deal of cleavage. Her face flamed from the embarrassment and the heat in Lex's eyes.

His face was inches from her chest. Her semi-exposed chest. The urge to press his head between her breasts made her hands shake.

"You're hair looks good curly. You should wear it like that more often." His voice snapped her back to the task at hand.

"Thanks. I think. I don't have a mirror so I can't tell if you're just trying to make me feel better or not."

"Honey, trust me you'll never have to wonder how I feel. What you see is what you get."

She let that slide and focused instead on picking little bits of hair through the bag. She'd never actually done this before, but she'd seen it done a hundred times.

"So tell me more about this ministry place. Is it like a nunnery where only women are allowed?"

His breath blew across her chest and her nipples hardened. Thank God her bra was padded or her nipples would stand out through her T-shirt, right next to Lex's lips. His full, sexy lips. Her knees turned to water as a warm glow radiated up from between her legs.

"Nothing like that. Have you heard of The Great Hope Ministry?"

"Isn't that the mission from that guy on TV? He's always asking for money."

"That's the one. About five miles from here is his headquarters. There's a shuttle bus that drops people off every half hour. I thought I could mingle with them and go in for a look around but almost every one of them is either ancient or female."

"That makes sense. Most men are at work during the day so the women and retirees are the only ones around to attend prayer services." Like her Aunt Betty.

"No kidding. I know why it's like that, but it doesn't help me to get in there. I'm going to have to go back at night and try to slip in without anyone noticing."

Jane's heart dropped to her toes. "Isn't that dangerous? I mean, what if they catch you? You can't very well say you snuck in to listen to the service. They must know who you are too."

"It's not the best idea I've ever had."

She took an unsteady breath before blurting out, "What if I go instead?"

"The thought crossed my mind. But are you sure you know what you're in for? Ouch! Be careful with those tweezers."

"Sorry." Her mind ran a thousand miles a second. What had made her volunteer for something like that? She jabbed him a few more times before slipping on the gloves and applying the dye. "Sit near the fire so that can dry properly." Jane peeled off the plastic gloves and washed her hands with a baby wipe.

He sat quietly by the fire while she gathered the garbage, her thoughts twisting this way and that. Aunt Betty's face flashed in her mind, urging her to help any way she could.

"I want to help. You're right that I don't know what I'm in for, but I'm smart. I think I can figure things out quickly enough."

Lex stared at her without saying anything for a minute. His eyes lasered into hers and she felt like he was assessing her. "You don't have to do this," he said at last. "I don't want to force you into anything over your head."

"I've been over my head since you popped up in the backseat of my car."

"True, but you haven't been in the thick of things. The ministry has guards and razor wire. I don't think they want interlopers."

"Do you want my help or not? If I go in and get the floor plan it would help you to know where to go when you broke in. Wouldn't that save you time?"

Why was she arguing about this with him? He was right,

she wasn't trained for this type of stuff. Why was she insisting on going?

Because she hadn't been able to help Aunt Betty in time. Maybe she could save someone else's aunt from losing her life's savings.

He tapped his chin speculatively. "You wouldn't try to do any Nancy Drew crap? You'd just go in and attend the prayer service then leave?"

"Of course." Her stomach clenched with nervous excitement.

"Let me think about it."

That was better than no. She was sure she could work him around to her way of thinking.

And if she could be brave enough to go on a secret mission, maybe she could scare up enough courage to talk him into something else.

Chapter Nine

"I still don't like it. I can't even slip a wire on you in case you need to be extricated in a hurry. I'd feel better if I went with you."

"Which would defeat the purpose of me going in the first place."

Lex had been drilling her on how to behave and what to look for until she was ready to stab herself with a stick just to relieve the tedium.

"I know. Damn, I hate this." He paced in front of the fire like a caged tiger.

"Do you think I should get some better clothes first? All I have are these jeans and a few cotton shirts. I'm not exactly dressed for church."

"You're fine. The women your age all wore jeans. It's not like going to Sunday Mass. The older women were dressed up, but they do that to go to the supermarket. From what I observed, it seemed like most of the younger women were housewives swinging in while the kids were in school or something. You'll fit in perfectly in your Wal-Mart wardrobe."

"Great." She felt about as attractive as a dishrag.

How unfair was that? Lex wore the same cheap clothes she did yet he looked hot. Very hot.

Jane licked her lips and tried not to stare at him as he paced back and forth in front of her. He was made for firelight. It gilded the harsh planes of his face and turned him into a Greek god. Even in his frustration he radiated sensuality.

She'd never felt such a constant sexual ache before. Every time he came within a foot of her, every nerve ending stood at attention. It was like they were electrically charged and every time their hands so much as brushed, lightning struck.

"What do you know about self-defense besides kickboxing?"

"I've taken some self-defense courses. I work a lot of nights and wanted to be able to defend myself if I got mugged." He didn't need to know she was working pro bono at the battered women's shelter at night instead of at her practice.

"Show me whatcha got."

"What do you mean? Right here?" She glanced doubtfully at the pebble and acorn-strewn ground. If he tossed her on her butt it wouldn't feel very good.

"I'm not asking you to do a gymnastics routine, I just want to see if you can break out of basic holds. You don't have to beat anyone up, just get free so you can run away."

"Oh, okay." She crossed the clearing away from the fire and searched her mind. How did one demonstrate self-defense techniques? "I'm not sure what you want me to do," she finally admitted.

"If I grab you around the throat, how would you get out of it?" He stood behind her and wrapped his arm around her neck. She could feel the solid length of him pressed against her from calf to shoulders and blood rushed through her like a tidal wave.

"Come on, princess, what would you do?"

Relying on muscle memory more than intellect, Jane

turned her head to relieve the slight pressure against her larynx. Once her air supply was no longer compromised, she jabbed her elbow into Lex's gut, stomped on his little toe and spun out of his grasp.

"Ouch! You didn't have to really crush my foot you know."

"Sorry, I wasn't thinking I was just reacting."

He shook his foot and rubbed his stomach where she'd elbowed him. "No, that's good. If you stop to think you'll end up in trouble. You did the right thing. Although, I'm glad you're wearing those flip flops and not something with any weight to it or I'd have been in big trouble."

Her face flamed, but she didn't have time to wallow in embarrassment because he came at her again, this time grabbing her wrist.

"Now what?"

Jane aimed a kick to his groin, which he neatly sidestepped.

"Don't go for the jewels, men expect that and naturally guard the boys. Aim for the knee or ankle. If you take out their knee then they can't chase after you."

She mumbled something she hoped sounded like assent. The smell of the fire was thick in the cool air. Lex's musky scent was even stronger. It drifted through her brain, clouding it with a fog of lust. Every time he touched her she thought her heart would pop out of her chest. She was so worked up she was surprised her hair wasn't standing on end.

Considering her lack of styling products, it very well could be.

"Okay, last one. What would you do if I grabbed both your arms like this?" He clutched her arms and stepped in so close she couldn't use her legs to kick him or step on his toes. The more she struggled, the tighter he held her.

What did her instructor say? When all else fails, fall. Jane let her body go limp, pulling Lex off balance and dropping them both to the hard ground. Lex twisted and landed on his side instead of squashing her beneath his body.

"Are you all right?" He leaned over her and ran his hands over her body, checking for injuries.

"I'm fine. Just a little winded from the fall. Sorry."

"Don't apologize, I told you to defend yourself. You did better than I expected. For a shrink, anyway."

"Thanks. That's quite a compliment, for an ex-Fed, anyway." He hadn't stopped touching her, but now his touch was more of a caress than an exam.

"Smart ass." His mouth drew closer to hers until it was a whisper away.

"It's not my ass that's smart." Why was she talking when his sexy lips were so close?

Jane's tongue flicked out to moisten her lips and she brushed his in the process. A bolt of heat speared her to the very core as he let out a groan and closed the scant distance between their mouths. This was no hesitant, exploratory kiss, oh no. This was an explosion of light and heat that rolled over Jane like a nuclear blast.

Lex didn't tease her or try to ease his way in. He stormed her walls and swept her along in his wake. His tongue captured hers, daring her to follow. Jane's toes curled from the amount of sheer pleasure surging through her body.

Her breasts were tender and achy under the steely wall of his chest. She ran her foot up the back of his leg, wiggling so he fit better between her legs. And oh, did he ever fit just right.

The hard length of his erection pressed against her much

softer mound, creating delicious friction even through their clothes. He slipped his hand under the hem of her shirt and stroked her stomach. Ever so slowly, he worked his way up her rib cage. Her heart stopped as she waited for him to reach her breast. When he gently cupped one plump curve, her heart resumed beating triple time.

The snap of the fire and the chirps of crickets were drowned out by the rush of blood pounding in her ears. The strong scent of pine and burning wood mingled with the completely male fragrance of Lex, heightening her arousal to an almost painful level.

Lex drew her lip between his teeth and sucked hard before kissing his way to her neck. Jane arched her back in abandon as he placed strategic nips along the nerve-filled tendons along her throat. With every touch, sparks ignited in her body and shot to her core.

A moan rumbled from Lex as he pushed her shirt and bra down, freeing her breasts for his voracious appetite. Jane clutched her fists in his shirt, holding on for dear life against the waves of pleasure threatening to sweep her away.

As Lex latched onto a nipple and sucked it into his mouth, Jane felt her womb contract with pleasure.

"I want to feel your skin against me," she gasped out.

"Happily."

Lex pushed up enough to yank his shirt over his head and toss it aside. Jane's mouth watered as the firelight danced over the ripples of his chest. She reached for him, eager to touch the naked skin and bulging muscles.

"Not so fast. Your turn." Lex's voice rumbled through her.

Jane felt a moment of embarrassment as she realized her top was bunched under her breasts. It was almost as if she had them displayed like a dessert tray. Then Lex moved closer and all she could think about was pressing herself against his gloriously bare chest. She whipped the shirt and bra off without another thought.

"Much better."

He rubbed his lightly furred chest across her nipples, creating bolts of heat at every point of contact. Jane ran her hands over his torso, amazed at how hard his muscles were, yet how soft his skin felt. The contrast reminded her of another hard yet soft area of a man's body and her hands shook as she thought of moving them south.

Her nails scraped along the ridges of his six-pack abs as her caress drifted lower.

And lower.

When she reached the snap of his jeans she hesitated. Did she really want to do this?

Yes!

Lex grasped her wrist and brought her hand lower to cup his length through his pants.

"Jesus, that feels good," he murmured, his lips pressed against the lower slope of her breast.

"You're telling me."

Lex kissed his way to her belly button, moving out of her reach. A whimper slipped from her lips at the loss of her plaything, but she soon found other amusements. Like the hills and valleys of his back and the bulging roundness of his shoulders. She wanted to touch every inch of him, feel his body against hers without any clothes between them.

He swirled his tongue in her navel and she arched her back to get closer to him. Her fingers tingled and her skin felt too tight to hold all the sensations coursing through her.

"Janey, we're approaching the point of no return here." He

ran his hand through his hair and clutched the back of his neck as if looking for something to keep him from touching her. "If you're going to say no, now's the time, because if I get your pants off you, they aren't going back on for a long time."

Her heart flipped over at the promise in his words. Did she want to do the right thing—like always—or see where these new and delicious sensations could take her?

"Promise?" Her libido answered before her brain could kill the party.

"Oh yeah." His teeth gleamed in the flickering light as he gave her a sexy grin. "Stay right there."

He kissed her again, guaranteeing she would be too boneless to move while he fumbled in one of the backpacks. Jane's drugged brain tried to stir itself enough to protest, but Lex was back at her side before it could fight its way through the sexual haze cocooning her.

He held a tiny foil packet in his hand. Had he planned this?

"I bought these because I use them to keep my weapon dry, not because I thought this would happen. Hoped, maybe, but I didn't plan for it."

"Really?" A warm glow spread through her at his words.

"Hell yeah. How can you doubt it?" He captured her lips in another mind-bending kiss, not giving her a chance to answer.

Jane was the one to break away this time. She wanted to taste him, to torment him with her tongue as he had done to her. The saltiness of his skin tasted better than any gourmet meal she'd ever had. His flat nipple raised into a tiny bump as she drew it into her mouth and nipped it. His musky scent drifted through her nostrils, swamping her senses.

"Holy Jesus!" Lex grabbed her shoulders and flipped her to her back. "You're killing me, sweetheart."

"Good." She felt powerful and unafraid. Brave even.

So brave, she didn't hesitate to pop the snap on his fly and unzip his jeans. Lex groaned, but did nothing to stop her from freeing his length.

"Oh my." She stroked his sex, loving the heavy heat of him.

"I think my brain just exploded but it feels too good to stop."

His knuckles grazed her belly as he unbuttoned her pants and pushed them down over her hips.

"Stopping is a very bad idea," she gasped. "Ouch." Something hard pressed into her back as Lex rolled her over to remove her jeans completely.

"Did I hurt you?"

"Not you, an acorn." She reached underneath to remove the offending item.

Before she could do more than chuck it aside, Lex scooped her into his arms and headed for the tent. "We can't have you distracted by acorns when there're so many other things to concentrate on." He squeezed a cheek of her rear end.

Jane felt giddy held in Lex's arms. His hairy chest rubbed against her breast and caressed her in a million places. This close she could see the stubble darkening his chin and see a drop of sweat glistening along his brow.

When they reached the tent, Lex released her legs so she slid down the entire length of his body. His unfastened pants slipped off as she rubbed against him.

"Let me take these off out here. There's not much room in the tent and I don't want to hurt you by accident."

She let her gaze drop to his pulsing erection and licked her lips. "Hurry."

"You'd better believe it." He kicked off his boots as she

turned to crawl through the zippered opening of the tiny tent. Seconds later, Lex followed with the flashlight.

"Dr. Farmer, do you have a tattoo on that delicious ass of yours?" He pressed her face down on the sleeping bag and stroked one globe of her behind.

"My one and only rebellion." She'd gotten the tiny rosebud in college and had regretted it almost immediately. Gerard had thought it completely tasteless and had urged her to get it removed.

She craned her head around to gauge Lex's reaction. His hot eyes practically scorched her skin. Boy was she glad she hadn't listened to Gerard.

"You're just full of surprises."

"Let me up and I'll show you some more." Where had this brazenness come from?

"Not yet. I want to examine your flower a little more." His fingers drifted between her legs and teased her entrance.

Shudders of need shook her frame. She had to bite her lip to keep from begging him to press his fingers deeper.

"That's. Not. My. Tattoo," she gasped out, trying to thrust back against his hand.

"I know. That isn't the flower that interests me right now."

He slid his finger deeper, stroking her most intimate spots. When his thumb grazed her sensitized nub, she couldn't hold back a cry. Her body shuddered and spasmed around his finger as he thrust it deeper inside her.

She was still recovering from the force of her flight when Lex rolled her over. He was fully sheathed and his eyes blazed in the low glow of the flashlight.

"Honey, I want to be gentle with you but I'm so keyed up I'm not sure I'll be able to."

"Don't. I'm not fragile, I won't break."

His thick legs spread her thighs wide to make room for him. Jane leaned up to lick his collarbone while he probed her entrance.

"Lord in heaven, I'm not going to last long," he growled as he slid all the way in.

Her inner muscles clenched around his length and another tremor shook her core as he moved in agonizingly slow circles. He leaned his weight on one elbow so he could cup her face in his hand.

"You're so beautiful." He teased her lips with the barest of touches. "So responsive. I want to make this good for you, but every gasp and touch makes me ready to explode."

Jane couldn't believe what she was hearing. He thought her beautiful? She was turning him on? Power surged through her.

"Me too." She planted her feet on the slippery sleeping bag and pushed upwards, driving him in even deeper.

Lightning rocketed along every cell as he threw his head back in surrender and drove into her. Lex clasped her hips in a punishing grip and thrust hard and fast.

Stars blossomed in her eyes as her world exploded. The last thing she saw was Lex's face as he reached his climax a second ahead of her.

⁗⁗⁗

"Are you cold?" Lex asked Jane when he could form words again. His brain was slowly returning to normal.

"Not a bit."

Jane stretched her arms over her head and her breasts brushed against his chest. Heat zipped down his torso straight between his legs.

So much for operating under normal brainpower. How long could the human mind last without blood going to it anyway?

Talk. He should try to talk to Jane. Women liked to snuggle and crap after sex, right? And Jane was a freaking therapist, she lived to talk about her feelings.

Good Lord, he'd rather face an armed opponent in his underwear than talk about feelings. Maybe he could fake it?

"That was most definitely worth the wait," Jane practically purred as she trailed her fingers through the hair on his chest.

"Glad to hear it. How long a wait has it been?"

"Too long. Since my divorce two years ago."

"You've gone two years without sex?" And she'd ended her dry spell with him. Was that good or bad?

Lex leaned up and secured the door flaps open to let the light from the fire in.

"Yup. A lady doesn't sleep around, you know."

"Huh?"

"Just one of the iron-clad rules my mother handed down. A lady doesn't chase a man, sleep with him before marriage or throw emotional scenes should she discover he's strayed."

"Are you kidding me?"

"I only wish I was. My mother didn't believe in outward displays of emotion."

Lex laughed. "I hope she never meets the women in my family. They can't sneeze without extreme emotion."

"I'd like to meet your family. They sound wonderful."

The wistfulness of her voice tugged at something in the region of his heart but he pushed it away.

"They are. It was hell having four older sisters, but I

wouldn't trade them for anything. Not that they'd let me anyway."

"I picture them as the type who would hug you as soon as you walked into the room then try to feed you."

"Pretty close. Throw in a few kisses and maybe a slap or two for not calling them and you've got the right idea."

"Do you know my father never once kissed me, or slapped me either for that matter? My parents weren't big on displays of affection. I sometimes wonder how they managed to get pregnant with me."

No wonder she was so skittish about physical contact. She wasn't used to it.

"That sucks. I may not have liked getting smacked when I did something wrong, but I got a lot more hugs and kisses than spanks. I always knew I was loved."

"I'll bet. Don't get me wrong, I know my mother loves me. She just really wasn't equipped to have a child. She doesn't like noise or disruptions to her routine."

"Sounds like your house was a lot of laughs."

"Yeah, well, on the positive side I went to all the best schools and had private tutors for tennis, dance, piano and French."

"Can you play piano?"

"Not a note. I have no musical ability whatsoever and even less rhythm. And I only know enough French to make sure I don't order snails at a restaurant."

"That's not a bad skill to have. I just got back from Paris and could've used someone to let me know what the hell I was eating. One night I ended up with pig's foot by accident."

Jane laughed out loud, and her whole face lit up.

"It's not funny. I saw *'pied du porc'* on the menu. I

recognized *'porc'* as pork so I ordered it. Let me tell you, I was more than a little surprised when the waiter came and there was a hoof on my plate."

"I'm sure it was a shock." Jane gasped with laughter.

"Laugh all you want. If I'd had had you with me I wouldn't have made that mistake."

The idea of going away with Jane when there weren't guys shooting at them sounded very tempting. What would it be like to stroll along the Seine with Jane instead of hiking through the woods of Pennsylvania?

Damn good, probably.

Jane's foot slipped along the inside of his leg. Her silky thigh brushed along his hairy one and his body stirred to life. He released a harsh breath as her hand stroked his growing length.

Although, lying in a miniscule tent with her wasn't all that bad either.

Her tiny tongue flicked out to stroke his nipple and his blood caught fire. That was the only way he could explain the surging heat rushing through his veins.

"You know, I've never been on top before." Jane straddled his hips and gazed down on him with sloe eyes.

"Then it's about time you tried." He barely had time to fumble on a condom before her wet heat surrounded him.

She threw her head back with a gasp. "I just love new experiences."

Chapter Ten

A slap on her naked butt woke Jane out of the best sleep she'd ever had, despite the fact she was sleeping on the ground. Lex leaned over her with a cup of coffee held just out of her reach.

"Come on, sleepy head. It's a long hike to the shuttle stop and I want to get an early start." He handed her the coffee and backed out of the tent.

Jane drew the sleeping bag up to her chin while she blew over the rim of the cup to cool the coffee for her first sip. Her brain was a jumble of memories and doubts tumbling around for supremacy. Lex hadn't appeared to be changed in the least by their lovemaking.

She felt as if the whole world had tilted on its axis. Not only had she been brave enough to have sex with Lex, she initiated it the second time around.

The third time was a mutual decision.

Maybe for him last night had been just another night in a long string of affairs, but for her it was like climbing Mount Everest. Only a lot more fun. She'd faced her fears of intimacy. Heck, she'd obliterated them. All this time she'd thought the reason she hadn't achieved orgasm was because of her inability to relax and enjoy sex. Now she knew better.

It didn't have as much to do with her inabilities as it did

her partner. Lex had enjoyed touching her before, after and during sex. He'd feasted on her body to the point where she had raw spots along her breasts and thighs from his razor stubble.

No wonder she'd never had an orgasm with Gerard. He'd treated her body like it was an investment and if he handled it too much it would lower the value.

Maybe she wasn't the one with intimacy issues after all.

"Come on, Janey. Get moving!" Lex shouted.

"I'm coming! Keep your pants on." She slipped on a spare shirt and a clean pair of undies before she wiggled out of the tent and stood. Her jeans and bra were still on the ground where Lex had stripped them off.

"That's not what you said last night."

Her face flamed as Lex ogled her bare legs. Memories of what Lex looked like without his pants made her knees weak. He must have recognized the lust burning in her eyes because he dropped the pan he was washing and strode over to her.

His lean hips pressed against her as he drew her within the circle of his arms. "We can always skip this mission and stay in bed all day." He nuzzled her neck seductively.

"I thought you needed inside information?" She'd meant to sound firm but her voice was breathy, husky.

"I do, but there are other things I'd rather get inside of right now."

Jane's muscles turned to water and she seriously contemplated his seductive offer. It would be much more fun to explore Lex in the light of day than it would be to go on some creepy mission. And she really should make sure she'd totally faced down her fears of intimacy...

"No. If we don't do this now we might not get another chance. I should go down there today." She stepped away from him and tried not to moan at the loss of contact.

"I hate that you're right. You'd better get dressed then, because if you flaunt your sexy bod in front of me much longer I won't give a damn either way."

A secret smile lifted the corners of her mouth. It was terribly shallow of her to be so happy that he liked her outward appearance instead of her intellect or her personality, but it felt darn good. No one had ever accused her of flaunting anything before.

While she cleaned up and got dressed, she snuck peeks at Lex whenever she could. His behavior confused her. The psychologist part of her didn't understand why he hadn't pulled away after the night of intimacy. Men just did that as a matter of course. It was a standard male pattern to step back, only Lex didn't show any signs of re-evaluating their relationship.

In fact, she was the one who needed some breathing room and wanted some alone time to figure out what was going on between them. As much as the memories of last night's hormone fest urged her to wrap her arms around Lex's muscled torso and rub up against him like a cat in heat, her brain was backpedaling like mad.

She knew she thought too much and analyzed things to death, but she couldn't stop the frantic spinning of her brain. Was last night just a one-time thing? Did she want it to be a one-shot deal?

And the sly voice in the back of her brain asked perhaps the scariest question of all. *When could they do it again*?

"You ready, Janey?" Lex's voice right behind her snapped her out of her thoughts.

Her face flushed as she remembered that same voice whispering hot, sexy words against her neck and breasts. And thighs.

116

How was she ever going to hike down the hill when her legs had the musculature of over-cooked spaghetti?

"Y—yes. I'm ready. I just wanted to make sure my blisters were covered before I put my sneakers on again."

"Are you sure you're going to be able to handle this?"

"I have two pairs of socks on over the bandages so I should be fine."

"That's not what I meant. Are you going to be able to go into that building alone?"

The doubt in his eyes brought her back up straight. He might no longer think she was a prude, but he still thought she was some hothouse flower.

"I might not be a super spy, but I think I can go into a building with several elderly women and housewives and come out unscathed. Like you said, all I'm doing is getting the floor plan, not trying to sneak into someone's office."

"You damn well better not try to sneak into anyone's office. I'm serious, no Nancy Drew crap. Just get in, take a tour or whatever they offer and get the hell out. I'll be watching you the best I can from a distance. Don't do anything stupid."

"I assure you, I may be many things, but stupid isn't one of them."

Lex swore under his breath and spun on his heel. Jane's heart beat furiously as he bent over to retrieve his gun and tuck it into the waistband at the small of his back. She abhorred violence, always had, but something about the danger surrounding Lex absolutely turned her on. It was probably a primitive response of her subconscious to a protector. Whatever it was, it was incredibly powerful.

Had she changed so much in such a short period of time? How had she gone from a respected therapist who was a card-carrying pacifist to an amateur spy who got turned on by a man with a gun?

If Lex hadn't climbed into the back of her car, would she have ever thought about going after the man who stole Aunt Betty's money herself instead of depending on the police to apprehend him? Not a chance.

And she'd never have faced her fears of intimacy and slept with Lex either. Which would have been a crying shame.

Another wave of heat made her tremble.

Focus, Jane. She was about to go on a semi-dangerous mission and all she could think about was the fabulous way Lex filled out his jeans.

"C'mon. I scoped out the nearest shuttle stop. I want to get you there a little early so you can mingle with some of the other women. Don't be obvious, but try to find out what goes on at the mission. See if you can find out why they have guards and barbed wire surrounding the compound."

"I'm a trained therapist. I'm pretty sure I can get information without browbeating the little old ladies." She pulled her sweatshirt over her head and held out her hand for Lex to lead the way. The sooner they got started, the sooner they could come back.

80CB

Lex watched Jane climb on the bus with his heart in his throat. There was no turning back now and it scared the hell out of him.

What had he been thinking of to let her go into that viper's pit by herself? If she got hurt it would be on his head. She was a freaking civilian and he'd allowed her to go into a potentially life threatening situation.

His father must be rolling over in his grave. Men took care of women. They didn't put them in danger.

The bus put-putted away, sealing Jane to her fate. All he could do now was watch and pray he hadn't mistaken the amount of danger involved.

Lex slipped the strap to the binoculars over his head and headed to the compound. By cutting through the woods, he could beat the bus to the mission and be in place when Jane arrived.

His thoughts wandered as he dodged the trees in his path. He still couldn't believe he'd had sex with his uptight neighbor last night. Good sex. Hell, great sex, even.

When he'd landed on top of her, all he could think about was exploring the soft curves pressing into him. Who'd of thought one touch and she'd go off like a rocket? Under that prim and proper exterior, Jane Farmer was a firecracker. And wouldn't that observation throw her for a loop?

Or maybe not. She'd held up a lot better than he'd expected. Now that he'd gotten to know her, he was willing to admit he might have been wrong about her. She wasn't as much uptight as she was shy.

At least at first. His groin tightened as he remembered her shyness melting away in the wee hours of the morning. She'd seemed so damn...surprised by that first orgasm. Could she have been married all those years and never had one? Lex couldn't suppress a smug smile. Jane might be the marriage counselor, but he'd shown her a thing or two about male/female relationships.

Maybe that's why she'd been so dazed this morning? He was used to women clinging to him the morning after. If not clinging, at least trying to find out when they could see him again.

Even though he'd caught Jane blushing—a sure sign she was thinking about last night—she hadn't said a word about it. She didn't seem to want to talk about last night either. That alone was a freaking miracle.

Or maybe a warning signal?

Did she just want to forget about it? He knew the sex had been good for her. He had the scratch marks to prove it. But then why had she chosen to go on the mission instead of spending the day seeing how many positions they could try?

Not that he'd have agreed to that anyway. He needed the intel so he could figure out what Sarah had gotten him into. What kind of woman wanted to spend the day snooping when she could be having screaming orgasms?

One who had gotten all she needed last night?

Could Jane have been using him? For sex? The idea was so preposterous it was almost funny. Isn't that what she accused him of doing? Using women then discarding them? It would be way too hypocritical of her to turn around and do the same thing.

Except, it'd be just like her to justify it because she thought he was a playboy.

A tight knot clenched in his gut. If she thought she could just screw him and then throw him away, she was in for a big freaking surprise.

Breathing heavily from more than just the run, Lex crested the last rise and secured a position just as the shuttle pulled into the circular driveway. A few housewives got out first and hurried to a doorway off to the side. Several elderly women shuffled out next, chattering amongst themselves as they headed to the main doorway.

Where the hell was Jane? His heart beat against his ribs like a snare drum. Could the guys who were after them at the hotel have recognized her and dumped her before they reached the compound?

No way. With her brown curly hair and sunburned face she looked nothing like herself. The jeans and baggy sweatshirt were so different from her normal, tailored attire it was a better disguise than a fat suit. She looked like a slightly frumpy housewife who'd never heard of makeup, forget high fashion.

Still, his nerves wound tighter and tighter until he saw her helping an older woman off the bus. She smiled and chatted with a couple of the old biddies as they strolled into the building. If he hadn't recognized her sweatshirt he might not have picked her out from among the other women in the group.

It looked like she'd actually listened to him when he'd coached her about changing her stride and the way she held herself. Instead of her stick-up-her-ass march, she shuffled along with slumped shoulders and loosely swinging arms.

If she could remember to slouch when she sat instead of looking like she had a steel bar for a spine, she'd be totally unrecognizable.

He hoped.

When she reached the door, she held it open for the others, smiling and nodding as they passed by. Briefly, her eyes scanned the tree line. Lex swore, afraid she'd point out his location to anyone watching her. His fears were for nothing because she slipped onto the tail end of the estrogen parade without a hitch.

As the door shut behind her a cold fist closed around his heart. She was on her own now and there was nothing he could do to save her. Giving up control was never easy for him, but right now it about killed him.

He just hoped his lack of control wouldn't kill her.

Chapter Eleven

"Margret, have you brought us a new member for our flock?"

Jane tried not to pull away as the skinny man grabbed her hand and held onto it. Charisma oozed from him and every eye in the hallway was glued to his face. Nausea churned in Jane's stomach as she feigned a smile.

"Oh yes, James Robert. This is Barbara and she came all the way from New York to hear your message." The elderly woman Jane had befriended practically gushed. "She's looking for the true path."

"Then you've come to the right place, my dear. Welcome to the Great Hope Ministry."

"Thank you. I've watched you on TV and I just had to come see you in person." She thought about fluttering her lashes but didn't want to push it so she just smiled shyly.

"God has indeed brought you here. I'd love to talk with you further, but I must prepare for the service. I hope you'll sit with me afterward and we can discuss your spiritual journey?"

"I'd love to."

About as much as she'd love to grow hair on her teeth.

An audible sigh went through the gathering as James Robert strode down the hall.

"Isn't he marvelous?" Margret asked, her eyes shining brightly.

"Oh yes. An angel sent down to Earth." Jane hoped no one caught her sarcasm.

"Indeed. Do you know, before James Robert put me on the true path I spent my days watching television and waiting for the phone to ring? After my husband died, I didn't know what to do with myself. The Great Hope Ministry changed all of that. Now I have a purpose in life. Helping others to find the light."

Margret's eyes shone with a fanatical gleam. Jane's queasy stomach roiled as the woman continued to sing his praises.

"James Robert saved me from the inside out. Before he laid hands on me, I had to take six different pills every morning and night."

"Really? What for?" Jane tried to hide the sudden lurch of fear that slammed into her.

"Oh, high blood pressure, high cholesterol, high blood sugar, you name it. I was on so many medications I couldn't keep them straight. But not any more."

"No?"

"Nope, not a one. James Robert said that the doctors only prescribed them to make more money. He told me I should donate the money I save from buying my medications to the starving in Africa, so that's what I did. And I've never felt so good. I don't get sick to my stomach or light headed any more. It's a miracle."

Luckily, Jane was saved from forming a response by their arrival at the meeting room. She didn't think she'd be able to gush about what an angel James Robert was without vomiting. That bastard was stealing their medication money.

And apparently, they loved him for it.

The enormous meeting room was already filled with people. There were decidedly more women then men, and many of them were far into their eighth decade. They appeared well off. Jane recognized wealth when she saw it. The cut and quality of their clothes screamed "old money." Even though there were several other women dressed in jeans, Jane felt positively gauche.

Margret led her to a row of seats right up in front and Jane wanted to hide from all the eyes burning holes into her back. She clutched her hands together, more scared than she was willing to admit.

Before long, the lights dimmed and the murmured conversations around her quieted. A single glowing light shone down on a pulpit and James Robert stepped up to the microphone. He wore a white robe over his clothes and his white hair gleamed like a halo in the light.

The room vibrated with energy as he gazed out on them. Logically Jane knew he couldn't see her because she was in the darkened audience and he was in the light, but she still felt like he stared right at her. By the sighs coming from the women behind her, they felt the same way.

"Brothers and sisters, let us pray." He raised his hands high and closed his eyes.

Jane pretended to close her eyes as well, but she peeked through slit lids to gauge the effect he had on the crowd.

It was downright scary.

In the dim light she could see expressions of rapture and devotion on the faces of the women nearest to her. They had their eyes closed and they swayed with his intonations.

A tremor of fear snaked through her and goose bumps chased over her arms. This wasn't a congregation. It was a cult.

As he continued to preach from the pulpit, she sensed the audience hanging on his every word. The charisma she'd noticed earlier seemed to intensify the longer he spoke.

"You must cast out that which offends the Lord! Isn't it written that there is no place in heaven for a rich man?" He waved his arms wildly and the crowd murmured their agreement.

Anger began to replace the fear that had taken root. He was no better than a con artist. She could see where his prayer service was leading. Praise the Lord and pass the collection plate.

A smooth talking "preacher" had conned her aunt out of her entire retirement fund. Aunt Betty had thought she was helping the missions in Haiti, and had almost gone into bankruptcy before Jane stopped it.

The snake had gotten away with thousands of dollars from gullible old women. The police had told her he'd disappeared without a trace. The money was probably in offshore accounts and would never be seen again.

Red-hot rage filled her as black-clad ushers walked to the front of the room and passed baskets around. The light was too dim for her to get a good look, but she was pretty sure she saw a handful of fifties in the basket that went past her.

A quick glance around showed other baskets filled to overflowing. There were easily fifty people in the room. If each of them tossed in a fifty, that was over two thousand dollars in one shot. If he did this every day, not to mention what he got from his other services and his TV appearances, he must be pulling in hundreds of thousands of dollars a week.

There's no place in heaven for a rich man, unless he happens to be a preacher. Jane was so caught up in her anger, she didn't notice the service had ended until the crowd surged to their feet and clapped wildly as the lights came up.

Beringed hands reached for the preacher as he walked

through the masses on his way out the door. One woman burst into tears when he shook her hand in passing.

Jane wanted to throw up. This wasn't religion. This was showbiz.

The lights came up and everyone filed out of the meeting room. Margret had tears in her eyes and she dabbed at them with a tissue she pulled from her sleeve.

"What did you think, dear? Isn't he amazing?"

"I'm speechless." She smiled the best she could through stiff lips. "What do we do now? Where is everyone going?"

"Well, some folks are going to the phones. Their mission is to spread the word to those who may not have seen James Robert's television show."

Good God, he was more evil than she'd thought. He was a telemarketer.

"Others will go to the assembly room where they'll package up the materials people have ordered on line. The Great Hope Ministry offers a whole series of motivational videos and inspirational CDs as well as printed materials."

"Amazing."

"Isn't it though? My job is to help with the cooking and cleaning. I prepare lunches for the other workers and supervise the kitchen staff. It's not so different from what I did at home for forty years, but for a much better cause."

One of the guards stepped away from the wall and approached Jane and Margret. Jane's heart lurched and her hands trembled with nerves.

"James Robert desires the pleasure of your company in his sitting room."

"Oh, what an honor, dear. Have fun and maybe I'll see you on the ride back." Margret patted her hand.

"That would be lovely. Thank you for showing me around."

"It's part of my job as a traveler on the true path."

Jane smiled weakly and followed the guard down an empty hallway. She tried to memorize the route so she could report back to Lex. It wasn't easy to examine everything and maintain a vapid air.

The guard held the door open for her and then shut it as soon as she stepped through. The click sounded far more ominous than it should have.

The lavish room had a plush leather couch and two matching armchairs. A door, presumably to an office, was at the far end of the room across a stark white rug. The walls were blindingly white as well and the only decoration was a portrait of James Robert. The heavily framed picture made him resemble a martyred saint.

Anger and nausea roiled in her stomach as she looked at the picture. The artist had added a slight glow around his head to enhance the halo effect. Couldn't people see through his act? Did they really believe by giving him their hard-earned money they could buy their way into heaven?

Jane wasn't a religious person, but she was pretty sure God didn't have a checking account and a billing service.

She was too nervous to sit, so she paced the confines of the room. On the third lap the door burst open and James Robert strode in like he could walk on water.

"Did you enjoy the service? I could feel the love in the room. I hope you felt it too." He sat on the edge of one of the armchairs and focused his laser beam-blue gaze on her.

Jane sat nervously on a leather sofa. "It was very interesting. I don't think I've ever experienced anything like that before." She forced herself to smile. Her acting skills just weren't good enough for her to do more.

"I'm so glad. I hope you'll come back for another service."

His eyes roamed over her frame, as if assessing her. When she crossed her arms over her chest, he raised his eyes and smiled at her benignly.

"I'd love to come back." Jane had to grit her teeth to hide her real feelings. She'd rather eat paint than spend another minute with him.

"We have other activities here besides the services. Many of our flock join us for study and contemplation too."

"I didn't realize you had so many programs here."

"Oh yes, our interests are very diversified."

Again, his gaze roamed over her like he could see through her clothes. Bile rose in her throat as she searched for a way to leave the room without having to touch him again.

Just when she was about to claim a desperate need for the bathroom a woman stepped through the door and her stare zeroed in on Jane.

Instantly, a wave of fear and revulsion swept over her. The urge to run became almost overwhelming. Jane couldn't explain her feelings rationally, but it set her knees knocking all the same. The only other time she'd felt this violent a reaction to a person was when she was on the witness stand at a murder trial. One of her shelter clients had been killed by her husband and his eyes held the same chilling lack of humanity that this woman's did.

"Oh, Susie! Excellent, you're just in time to meet our new guest. Barbara, meet my wife Susie Beaupree."

"It's a pleasure to meet you." Susie's smile didn't quite reach her glacial eyes.

She held out her hand and Jane braced herself to shake it. It was all she could do to hide her reaction. Susie's hand was warm and dry, but instead of being comforting it reminded Jane of a touching snake.

"Likewise." Jane yanked her hand away as quickly as she could.

It wasn't that Susie was repulsive. In fact, she was very plain. She was the type of woman who would blend into the background—Which was probably what James Robert saw in her. With her dishwater-blonde hair and drab, buttoned-up dress, she was like a mud wren next to a peacock.

Jane couldn't wait to get out of the room. Every time she met Susie's gaze, it felt like someone walked over her grave.

"Thank you so much for your inspirational service and the invitation to come back. Unfortunately, I need to get home now."

James Robert wrapped an arm around his wife. "You're welcome. We hope you'll come see us again soon. One of my lieutenants will walk you to the shuttle. It's easy to get lost here if you don't know your way."

His laser-like eyes zeroed in on her and Jane felt the last ounce of nerve in her body fade. First, the wife gave her the heebie-jeebies, now the husband sized her up. If the lieutenant didn't come soon, Jane was bolting. She'd find another way to help Lex.

But would it be enough to save Margret and all the other women?

Jane forced herself to chat inanely with Jim Bob while she waited for the lieutenant. Cold sweat dribbled down her back as she forced herself to stay put. If she flew the coop it might make Jim Bob nervous and that would complicate things for Lex.

She could do this. She would do this. For Aunt Betty and all the other gullible women out there who wanted to be part of something good.

Finally, there was a polite knock and Susie stepped out of the way. Jane shuffled to the door where the guard waited. Her neck prickled and chills shook her. She fought the urge to hurry.

The sight of the short, white bus with "Great Hope Ministry" printed on the side was a welcome relief. It didn't matter that she'd have to squeeze her way inside with a bunch of strangers. She was desperate to get away from this place while she still had her sanity.

Chapter Twelve

Lex stared as Jane scrubbed herself with baby wipes. She'd been at it since the minute they returned to camp and hadn't let up for the last half hour. If she kept it up, she'd scour the skin from her bones.

He'd given her some space after she'd filled him in on what went on behind the closed doors of the ministry. She had an amazing memory and attention to detail and he was still trying to piece everything together.

"Tell me again, where were the other women going? The ones who got off the bus first?"

"They were going to the packaging room, I think. I didn't actually see them, but from what Margret said, that was where the assembly room was."

"I wonder why it was only the young women who went there?"

"Maybe because they're stronger? Some of the older women aren't very steady on their feet. Considering Jim Bob takes their heart medication money, he's probably afraid if he had them do any strenuous work they'd keel over."

Jane scrubbed her hands again. He'd never seen her so agitated before. What the hell had happened in there?

"Tell me more about the women."

"Like what?"

"What were they like? Did any of them talk to you on the bus?"

"Oh yes. They were all very friendly. I heard about the miracles James Robert performed and all his charitable work."

"Did you find out why he has guards and a barbwire fence?"

"Yes. He has a drug treatment center on the compound and the fence and guards are to keep addicts from trying to break out."

"Yeah, right. The guards patrol with military precision. You don't need that for junkies."

"I guess there's some drug activity in the area. When I asked about the fence, one of the women told me about a bust in the next town. Apparently, some kids were delivering crystal meth along with their pizzas and sold to an undercover cop. They never found the lab or the dealers, from what I gather."

"What do you want to bet that James Robert has a lab somewhere on that compound? Did you smell anything? A strong chemical odor or like something was burning?"

"No, nothing like that. But I was only in a small area."

Jane had finally stopped trying to clean herself and now huddled by the fire. She looked scared and angry at the same time. His heart went out to her. He imagined it wasn't easy for her dealing with the dregs of humanity, especially for the first time.

"I guess I wasn't much help," she said, staring into the fire.

"Are you kidding me? You found out where James Robert's office was, gave me a partial floor plan, got the schedule of services and found a possible reason for why he killed Sarah. You did more in two hours than I've done in the last two days."

"Really?"

"Really."

"I was thinking I could go back tomorrow and maybe get a better look around if you want."

"No. You've done enough."

"But—"

"But nothing. If you go back tomorrow they might suspect something. Now if you're done cleaning, I want you to pack up your stuff while I take down the tent."

"We're moving?"

"Yup. I don't want to take any chances someone followed you from the shuttle."

"But I thought you covered our trail? That was why you zigzagged all over the forest, wasn't it?"

"Yes, but you can never be too careful. Come on, we don't have much daylight left."

Lex turned his back on her and rolled up the sleeping bags. He wanted to move closer to the car in case they had to make a run for it. Something about this whole set up had his gut instincts screaming bloody murder and he wanted Jane as far away from it as possible.

When did she go from being a pain in his ass to being someone he wanted to protect? Even at the risk of blowing the mission? He hadn't been completely honest with her. It would be helpful if she returned to the ministry. And the risk was pretty minimal, but he couldn't chance it.

Waiting for her to emerge from the building today had been one of the hardest things he'd ever done. That could be why he was in such a hurry to break camp—he needed to feel in control again. At least by covering their trail he was doing something instead of watching Jane put herself in danger.

He refused to think about why her safety meant more to him than finding Sarah's murderer. He was sure he wouldn't like the answer.

℘℘

Jane tried to hide her trembling hands in the sleeves of her overlarge sweatshirt as she huddled by the fire at their new campsite. She didn't want Lex to know how scared she'd been.

He'd been so proud of her for going into the ministry. She didn't want to blow that by falling apart like a frightened child. Even though that's exactly how she felt.

She'd been relieved when he'd nixed the idea of going back to the compound. Going into that hellhole was the very last thing she wanted to do, but he'd been so full of praise for her she'd had to offer. It felt good to have him compliment her on her bravery. It made her want to do more to impress him.

And wasn't that the scariest thought of all?

"Is there anything else you can think of that didn't seem right? Any little thing?" Lex asked, handing her a cup of coffee.

"We've gone over this a hundred times. I've told you everything I saw."

"I know, but something's funky and I can't put my finger on it. Don't confine yourself to the facts, give me your impressions or gut feelings. Even if they're way off base they might give me something to go on."

"Well, there was something—"

"What?"

"This is just my opinion, but I think it's valid. It seemed to me most of the women who went off before the service might be abused."

"Explain." His gaze bored into her but he didn't discount her observation.

"I don't think Jim Bob is the one abusing them, but they had the look of women who'd been victims of domestic violence."

"I didn't pick that up."

"Most people don't. I've counseled a lot of abused women and they all have a... I don't know, a wariness in their eyes. It's the way they guard their actions as if expecting a blow even when no man is around."

"And all the women that went to the packaging room were like that?"

"Not all of them, but I'd say the majority, yes."

Lex grunted and poked at the fire. "Do you think Jim Bob's wife—what's her name—Susie? Did she look abused to you?"

Jane couldn't hold back the shiver that skated down her spine. "No, she definitely didn't look abused."

"I thought you said she was a mousey looking thing? You act almost afraid of her."

"She was mousey. But she had these eyes that looked right through you. James Robert was smarmy, but Susie scared me."

"She was probably protecting her meal ticket. Sounds like old Jim Bob has a wandering eye."

"That's for sure. After being in his presence for five minutes I wanted to take a burning hot shower. In bleach."

Lex threw his head back and laughed. His rumbling chuckle soothed her jangling nerves and chased some of the chill from her bones.

"It's not funny. The guy gave me the absolute creeps."

"I believe you. I'm impressed that you managed to get so much information out of him even though you wanted to spit in his eye. You've come a long way from the frightened woman who almost drove us into a tree when I popped up in her back seat."

"You beast, you scared the living daylights out of me. But you're right. I'm much stronger now."

She hadn't realized it until she said the words, but it was true. Sure, she still got scared, but she'd stopped running away from the things that frightened her and that was a huge step.

If only Gerard could see her now. Ha!

"What's that smile for? You look like the cat that ate the canary."

"I was just thinking that now if I caught my husband having sex with his secretary I'd throw the coffee pot at him instead of quietly backing out of the room."

"Sounds like someone was giving a little more than dictation?"

"Oh yes. My ex-husband Gerard threw away our marriage and our practice so he could boink our secretary. On the couches I picked out, I might add. He said it was my fault because I wasn't passionate enough."

"What a charmer. You're better off without the loser."

"You have no idea." For the first time, she could smile when she thought about the night she found Gerard grunting and sweating over their secretary. Lex was absolutely right. She was so much better off without Gerard. And maybe, if she played her cards right, she'd be better yet.

Jane locked eyes with Lex and very slowly peeled off her sweatshirt. Her knees shook with nerves, but she could do this. She wanted to do this.

"Uh, what are you doing?" Lex asked as she knelt between his knees and reached for the snap on his pants.

"You're not very much of a playboy if you have to ask."

He sucked in a ragged breath as she freed him from the confines of his jeans.

"Maybe a better question would be, why are you doing this? If it's just to prove something, don't bother. I'm not your guinea pig." His eyes closed and his head dropped back as she trailed her tongue along his length. "Then again, I've always thought guinea pigs were kind of cute."

She stopped kissing him and waited for him to meet her gaze. "I'm doing this because you gave me a great deal of pleasure last night and I want to return the favor. I'm doing this because it gives me pleasure to touch you." She ran her hand along his hardness. "To taste you." She captured his tip in her mouth. "And because, for the first time in my life, I can."

"Works for me," Lex gasped.

℘☙

Lex stroked Jane's satiny back as she lay curled on her side against his chest. They'd zipped the two sleeping bags together and snuggled in them. The night might be cool, but Janey was nice and warm against him. After her actions in front of the fire, he didn't think he'd ever be cold again.

"When I was sitting in that meeting room, watching all those women throw their money at James Robert, I got so angry I'm amazed I didn't explode on the spot."

"It's hard to watch people throw their lives away."

"I was surprised. I never get angry. It's unproductive and just masks the emotions going on underneath."

"I get mad all the time. It's not masking anything."

"I'm not going to get into a psychological discussion with you. While I was there I thought about how any one of those women could have been my own mother...or aunt."

She grew quiet, but Lex didn't fill the silence. Something was on her mind and he needed to let her work it out.

"My Aunt Betty was taken in by a con man. Mother and I barely found out in time to save her. She lost everything and the man was never caught. I don't want that to happen to anyone else."

"Don't worry, babe, we'll stop Jim Bob."

He just wished he knew how he could do that without involving Jane.

Lex waited until he felt her breathing even out and her body relax in sleep. Jane would be pissed off if she found out what he was up to, but he had to do something. He couldn't let her take any more risks.

His breath puffed out in thin clouds of mist as he slipped out of the tent. He wasted no time dragging on his jeans and boots. Had he only just thought he'd never be cold again? Just went to show how sex screwed with a guy's brain.

Especially sex with Jane.

Her ex was a freaking idiot. If Jane was his wife, he'd never so much as look at another woman. Okay, he was Italian, so he'd probably still look, but he definitely wouldn't sleep with another woman.

What the hell was he thinking? Had he actually thought the W word without breaking into hives? They needed to finish this case and get back to civilization before he started picking wild flowers and writing sonnets. The thin mountain air must be messing with his mind.

The trip to the compound was quite a bit longer since they moved campsites, and sweat dripped down his back by the time he reached the fence. The guard on perimeter duty passed by, right on time. Lex had less than five minutes to scale the fence before the next guard turned the corner.

Thank God, the fence wasn't electrified. The razor wire was bad enough without chancing electrocution. His leather gloves would protect his hands to a degree, but he could easily slice an arm or a leg fatally if he wasn't careful.

He was very careful.

The second his feet hit the ground, he ducked and rolled to avoid the security camera. His heart thudded rapidly as he crouched in a doorway and waited to see if he'd been spotted.

No alarms went off and no grunts came running so he assumed he remained undetected. Now he just had to get to Jim Bob's office and hack into his computer for the evidence that corresponded with what Sarah had sent him. Piece of cake.

Lex made his way to the row of rooms Jane had told him contained Jim Bob's waiting room and potentially his office. He'd almost reached the end of the building before he spotted it.

The large walnut desk with the state-of-the-art computer had to belong to Jim Bob. He checked his watch. Two more minutes before the next guard arrived. He'd have to move damn fast to get into the office without getting spotted.

Adrenaline made his blood rush as he slid his fingers around the window frame looking for an alarm. Crap, it was wired. The seconds ticked away, increasing his chances of being caught with every heartbeat.

He'd almost figured out where the trigger point was when the spotlight on the corner of the building lit up the night. Spots danced in his eyes as he dove for the cover of a prickly shrub.

One of the guards ambled around the edge of the building, smoking a cigarette. He must have come out the back door and set off the motion-sensing lights. If Lex moved from the cover of the shrub before the light went out, his black clothes would stand out like a sore thumb.

He held his position, waiting for the guard to pass. Lex kept his eyes down so no hint of light could glint off them and alert the goon. There wasn't going to be enough time to re-wire the alarm. But if he broke the window, he wouldn't have time to hack into the computer.

Crap. He needed a plan B. Unfortunately, Jane was his plan B.

As he waited for the guards to move on their way he tried to find another way to get in that didn't put Jane at risk, but it was useless.

The pain in his legs from holding his crouched position was nothing compared to the pain squeezing his heart.

Chapter Thirteen

Jane stared at Lex like he'd lost his mind. He'd gone to the ministry last night without telling her. He could have been killed.

"So let me get this straight. The only reason you're asking for my help now is because you couldn't get in last night?"

"I wouldn't ask you at all if I had any choice."

"I see."

She really didn't want to go back to the Great Hope Ministry. Just the thought of facing James Robert again had her knees knocking with fear, but she'd do it. She had to.

And it wasn't just to prove something to Lex, but because it was the only way to stop James Robert. All night long, she'd had dreams of Margret having a heart attack because she refused to take her medication.

That bastard had to be stopped and she and Lex were the only ones who could do it.

No, she was the only one who could do it. Lex hadn't been able to get into James Robert's office last night. Jane hadn't even realized he'd left until she'd woken up alone.

"Can you think of another way to get me in there? I've racked my brain, but I can't come up with anything." Lex paced across their tiny campsite with barely leashed frustration.

"I can get into the office. I know how to work James Robert. For heaven's sake, I spent eight years studying human behavior. If I can't get him to leave me alone in there, no one can."

"I know that, but I don't have to like it." He took her hand lightly in his and traced circles on her palm with the pad of his thumb

"He has to be stopped. Whether or not he's involved with the drugs, we need to find a way to shut him down."

"You could be risking your life. Are you sure you're willing to do that?"

Her heart lurched. No, she really wasn't willing to die, but now that the tiny seed of strength inside her had bloomed, there was no going back.

"Yes. If for no other reason than he's suckering lonely grandmothers into quitting their medications so they have more money to give him. I owe it to my Aunt Betty. I couldn't live with myself if I just gave up and let him continue to destroy people's lives. Doing the right thing is worth taking the gamble with my life." She just prayed luck would be on her side for a change.

"I hate asking this of you."

"I know." She took a steadying breath. "How do you want to do it?"

Lex's eyes hardened. He was all business now. "I'll sneak in through the woods. You take the shuttle. Ask Jim Bob how you can donate money to his cause. Tell him you have a trust fund lying around collecting interest and you want to do something with it. That should get you in his office fast enough. When you get rid of him, open the window so I'll know you're in place. I'll sneak in that way. We'll get what we need and get the hell out."

"Just like that? If it's so easy, why couldn't you get in last night?"

142

"Because the window was alarmed, for one thing. The alarms should be off now. Also, during the day the guards aren't going to be as suspicious if they see someone walking around as they would if they spotted me at night. Not that I plan on them spotting me, but you get the idea."

"If you say so."

It still seemed dangerous to her, but she'd do it anyway. If this was the only way to stop James Robert from ruining people's lives, she'd do what she had to.

She released a pent up breath and stared him right in the eye so he wouldn't misunderstand her. "Thank you."

"For risking your life?"

"No, for trusting me." It meant more to her than she could say.

"Hey, I'm no idiot. I know better than to mess with a tough broad like you." He drew her close and wrapped his arms around her shoulders.

Laughter and tears spilled from her. "No one has ever thought I was tough before. I never thought I was tough before."

"Yeah, and you didn't think you were passionate either but I think we disproved that stupid idea more than adequately last night." He cupped her face in his strong hands and stared into her eyes.

Jane's heart flipped over and her pulse rate shot through the roof. "About last night—"

"Last night was beautiful. Now let's go get Jim Bob." He kissed her quickly on the lips and melted into the trees.

Jane remained stunned for another moment before she pulled herself together. Digging through the clothes they'd bought, she searched for something a little more dressy than her sweatshirt.

Her options were very limited. Finally, she settled on Lex's button-down shirt and tucked it into her jeans. She wished she had time to get some more appropriate clothes—James Robert might have a hard time believing she had a trust fund dressed like this—but she'd make do.

Releasing a quivery breath, she walked toward the shuttle stop. Lex's lemony scent drifted up from the collar of the shirt and memories from last night flashed through her brain. He hadn't given her a chance to say anything before he left, which might be a good thing.

What could she say? Last night was a unique experience for her. How could she tell him that she felt more comfortable with him after less than a week than she'd ever felt with her ex-husband after years of marriage?

That wasn't something she could admit. Thank God, he hadn't given her a chance to embarrass herself. He thought she was a strong, passionate woman. It wouldn't do a bit of good to let him know she was a nervous wreck who'd developed an attachment to him.

So much for being a "tough broad".

ℰℭ

"I know my boyfriend will be upset, but I need to give this money away. I want to have meaning in my life. I want to walk the true path." Jane sobbed into a tissue.

James Robert sat next to her on the arm of the leather chair and held her hand. Every once in a while he'd murmur a consoling platitude and stroke her shoulder. It was all she could do to keep from shuddering at his touch.

"The one true way isn't easy, dear."

"I want to do something with my life. I want to do more with my trust fund than go on vacations and buy stupid cars and boats. You're doing such wonderful things here. I want to be part of it." She looked up through tear-filled eyes and blinked rapidly, causing those tears to fall delicately down her cheeks.

A benevolent smile crossed his face and he crouched down in front of her. "Do you really mean that, Barbara? Do you truly wish to become a member of our flock? I don't want you doing anything in the spur of the moment. If it's your ardent desire to join us then I welcome you, but you have to honestly want it."

"Oh I do. I really do. I've been searching for something like this for so long."

"I'm happy to see you've found what's been missing in your life. Why don't we go into my office and you can sign the necessary papers?"

Jane looked down and wiped her face with the tissue to hide the exultation burning through her. *Yes!*

"Papers?" she asked when she had her emotions under control.

"Just a few formalities. You need to sign a release so that we can contact your bank to transfer the funds for the foreign missions. You do want to help the starving children overseas with your donation, right?"

"Yes, yes of course." *Yeah right.*

James Robert led her into the office and sat down behind his enormous desk. Jane saw him quickly minimize a document on the screen before he pulled some papers out of a file drawer.

"Now, if you have your bank account and tracking number handy, just put those down here. You'll need to sign at the 'X' and initial here and here," he said pointing to various lines on the pages. "This one is a release of liability that our lawyers insisted on using. It's a terrible thing when you have to take time away from God's work because of a greedy person's misguided need for money. Greed is one of the seven deadly sins, you know."

"Yes, I remember that from your sermon."

Jane held off signing the paper as long as she could. She had to find a way to get James Robert out of the office for a while so she could let Lex in through the window. What could she do to get him to leave her alone?

"I don't have my bank account number memorized, I'll need to look in my check book," she said at last.

"No problem, dear. Where is it? We can go get it right now."

"It's in my purse. Oh no! I left on the shuttle bus," she lied.

"Don't worry. We'll have one of the drivers bring it back."

"But what if they don't? What if someone stole it? How will I be saved then?" She sobbed into her tissue again.

"There, there. Dry your tears. I'll take care of everything. Just wait here while I have a word with my lieutenant."

Gotcha.

"Are you sure?"

"Absolutely." He patted her hand and slipped out of the office.

Jane got up and waited by the door. The slam from the waiting room rattled the walls and left no doubt James Robert had left. She scampered behind the desk and threw open the window.

Blood rushed through her veins so fast she could hear her heart pounding. Her hands shook as she brought up the document James Robert had minimized. It had a bunch of names like "Lucky Strike" and "Nobody's Fool" and numbers after them.

Jane had no idea what they were but she saved a copy on the little jump drive Lex had given her. Where was he? She
146

brought up the open file menu and clicked randomly, hoping something she saved would be what Lex needed.

"What have you got?" he whispered as he slid through the window like an eel.

How could such a big man move so quietly? He'd scared the hell out of her.

"I have no idea. I'm just saving everything I find. This was what he was looking at when I came in." She brought up the document. "Do you think those are drug names? They don't look like anything I've ever heard of before."

"Nobody's Fool? He's a horse. That's a betting sheet for horse racing."

"Oh for the love of God. He's robbing old ladies of their pensions to play the ponies?"

"Looks that way. Move over, I need to see what else is in there. Stand by the door and let me know if someone comes."

Jane slipped out from behind the desk and opened the door a crack. The sound of Lex's fingers on the keys was as loud and fast as machine-gun fire to her heightened senses.

"Crap. There's nothing here. Nothing."

"What do you mean?" Jane asked, turning to look at him.

"I see plenty of information about the ministry scam, but nothing like Sarah sent me. He must have that on a completely separate computer. Damn it! This isn't going to do anything but give him a slap on the wrist. There has to be something else." He rolled from the desk in frustration.

"There is, but you won't be here to find it."

Jane spun around and saw Susie pointing a gun at Lex. She stood in the doorway of what Jane had thought was a closet. Apparently it wasn't.

"Hello, Susie. Fancy meeting you here." Jane tried to edge

closer to Lex but stopped when Susie pointed the gun at her chest.

"I'm sure it's a big surprise." She gestured with the barrel of the gun for Lex to move out from behind the desk.

While Lex complied with her demands, Susie pulled a cell phone from her pocket.

"Tank, I need you in the office. Use the cellar stairs."

"This isn't really what you think," Lex said.

"Oh please. I'm not Jim Bob. I recognize an agent when I see one, Mr. D'Angelo."

"How do you know my name?"

"I have my sources," she said smugly.

Jane's heart pounded furiously and fear made sweat drip down her back. She was so stupid to think they could just slip in here and get the information without getting caught.

"I know all about EIS and what you do for them. The only thing I couldn't figure out was how the good doctor got involved. My sources had no information on her at all."

"That's because she's not involved. She was doing me a favor coming in here so I could find out what you were up to."

"Please. How stupid do you think I am? Do you think I didn't notice her working James Robert? That I didn't see her scoping the place out? I'm not so focused on her boobs that I couldn't see what was going on."

"And what exactly is going on? I know it's more than Jim Bob's shell game, but I can't figure out what."

Susie laughed at Lex, but it didn't sound like she was amused. There was an edge to her laughter that sent a shiver down Jane's spine.

"You have no idea what sort of shell game I'm playing. Forget what he's doing."

It looked like she was going to say more but an enormous man stepped into the doorway where Susie had come from. The same man who'd shot at them at the hotel.

They were so dead.

"Take them downstairs and tie them up while I try to convince that idiot to cut and run while we can. He's going to ruin everything."

Lex stepped in front of Jane as if to protect her. Tank took out a gun that looked ridiculously small in his mammoth paw and put it against Lex's head.

"If you don't want to see lover boy's head blown off don't try anything stupid. We're taking a little trip downstairs."

Jane's knees turned to water. Terror flooded her when Tank roughly yanked Lex's arm behind his back and pushed him toward the secret door. Sunlight glinted off the gun he held against Lex's head.

Jane was terrified this would be the last time she ever saw daylight.

Chapter Fourteen

"I'm so sorry. I should have been watching the other door. I thought it was a closet." Jane bit her lip while Lex struggled against the hard, plastic ties that held him to the chair.

Tank had taken them through a maze of underground hallways to a storeroom where he'd had Jane tie up Lex with the thick plastic ties. She'd tried to leave them on the loose side, but Tank had yanked them tight enough to cut into Lex's skin.

"Assigning blame doesn't do us any good right now."

"What are we going to do?" Jane winced as the wire ties dug into in her wrists. She was frightened enough to break her own arm if that's what took to escape. While Tank secured her to the chair, he'd whispered violent suggestions about everything he was going to do to her when Susie turned her back.

Panic rolled over her, but she refused to fall apart. No matter what Lex said, she knew it was her fault they were down here. But he was right, wringing her hands over her stupidity wouldn't solve anything. She needed to focus on helping Lex to get them out of here.

"Do you have any give to your ties? That bastard pulled mine so tight they're cutting off my circulation." The muscles of his arms bulged as he strained against his bonds.

Jane tugged at the plastic holding her wrists together behind her back. Abject fear had made her hands sweaty. "I can slide them up and down a little, but not much."

"It'll have to do. Try to rub the tie against the back of the chair to weaken it."

"Will that really work?" She felt around for something rough to work the binding against.

"Probably not, but it's better than sitting here doing nothing."

Great.

"What's that smell?" A strong chemical odor pervaded the cellar. It was so strong it burned her nostrils and made her eyes water.

She rubbed her hands harder, for all the good it did. Her arms ached from the awkward position and her wrists had started to bleed from the friction.

"Meth lab. You said the teens got busted for dealing crystal-meth. I'll bet Susie is the supplier."

The plastic tie wasn't weakening in the least, no matter how hard she rubbed the damn thing against the back of the chair. It was all she could to hold back a whimper of pain, but she kept going. What other choice did she have?

"I can't believe I didn't put it together before. The information Sarah grabbed was the distribution list. The names were the dealers Susie worked with and the amounts were what they owed her."

"But why here? Wouldn't it make more sense to operate closer to the city where there'd be a bigger demand?" Blood dripped down her hands, making it harder to hold the tie tight while she rubbed.

"No. Meth is the new suburban drug of choice. Labs are

easy to set up in basements and sheds. Kids in the 'burbs have a lot of money to spend on recreational drugs."

"That's terrible."

"Yup, but reality. Think this through. Susie had the perfect cover with Jim Bob's operation upstairs. The location was secure. She had manpower and could ship her product out with Jim Bob's promotional materials. What do you want to bet that some of those videos he mailed out didn't contain his message but a nice supply of meth instead?"

"Who would inspect a shipment coming from a Bible thumper like James Robert? She could send her drugs anywhere in the country without anyone the wiser. That's sick."

"But very smart."

"Why thank you, D'Angelo. I thought so too," Susie said.

She strode into the storeroom like a queen entering her throne room. Jane noticed a huge difference in her body language and the way she held herself.

When Jane had seen her before, Susie had appeared to blend in with the background. She'd played second fiddle to James Robert's charismatic personality.

Now she was in charge and proud of it. This was her operation, not her husband's and she wasn't bowing down to anyone.

"I have to admit, I'm pretty impressed that no one connected the drug activity to the arrival of the mission."

"That's because I convinced James Robert to start a drug treatment center and a drug prevention program as part of the mission."

"Pretty slick." Lex tipped his head towards her in a mock salute. "That not only diverted attention from you, but also gave you a list of potential customers. I didn't think Jim Bob was a good enough actor to pull off that big a scam."

"He isn't. He thinks the drug treatment program is for real. The lab is my doing. He has no idea what goes on down here."

"I can't believe that. This is a large operation. He has to know something's going on." Lex said.

"Nope. He thinks this is nothing but storage. He has no idea where the money comes from. I handle all the finances that have to do with the facility so he doesn't suspect a thing. In his head, he's a great preacher like his grandpappy was, traveling around the country preaching his message to the masses." She laughed derisively. Her grip on the gun loosened slightly, but she didn't put it down.

"So you play the submissive little wife to his shining star," Jane said. "It must be hard to know that you're really the brains of the operation while he gets all the attention and adoration."

"Don't try to analyze me. It won't work. I couldn't care less what he or his idiot flock believes. I use him and his network for my operation. It works to my advantage for him to believe I'm ignorant."

"How did Sarah manage to find out about this set up?" Lex shot Jane a warning glare. He didn't want Susie's attention on her.

"That bitch! She betrayed me." She bit back whatever else she was going to say with a look of such extreme pain Jane couldn't miss it.

She'd seen that expression hundreds of times on the faces of her marriage therapy clients. That was the expression of love betrayed. The realization hit her at the same time her hand slipped out of the stretched wire tie. It was all she could to keep her face blank and not clue Susie in.

"You trusted her, didn't you? She saw right through James

Robert and knew you were the one who was in charge. You must have loved her a lot to trust her with the truth. And she betrayed you by stealing the information and running away."

Susie's face blanched as if Jane had struck her. Lex sucked in a harsh breath.

Susie turned on him. "Does it surprise you that your lover slept with other women? That she preferred girls to you?"

A stab of pain struck Jane straight through the heart. Sarah had been Lex's lover. That's why he came here, to avenge her. Oh God, it made so much sense now. He was compensating for not being able to save her by completing the last mission she was on.

"Sarah and I hadn't been lovers for years. If she started playing for the other team it was long after we split up." His eyes bored into Jane's as if trying to explain it to her too. "It wasn't like I was in love with her."

"Then why did she send you a package? Huh? Explain that?"

"I don't know. Maybe because she trusted me? Or maybe she suspected you had someone on the inside at EIS?"

The smug smile was back on Susie's face. "She didn't have any idea I had a line into her precious employer. Not that it did me any good. I didn't find out she was an EIS agent until after she took off with the information. If I had found out sooner none of this would have happened."

Jane had no idea what Susie was talking about, but she didn't care. The pins and needles stabbing her hands had finally subsided and she could move her fingers without pain again.

"I don't understand why you'd want to hurt an agency that saves children. EIS had nothing to do with you until Sarah came here. Why did you target them?" Jane asked, trying to keep Susie's attention off Lex.

"Don't be so naïve. EIS doesn't just rescue children. They have government contracts and contacts all over the country. They're tapped into information from DEA, ATF and the FBI. My source was able to tell me when multi-agency groups were getting ready to make a bust so I could abort shipments. EIS has undercover agents gathering information for the government worldwide. And it was a lot easier getting someone into the EIS office than it would have been getting them into a government position."

"Who's the mole?" Lex asked. A muscle in his jaw twitched and the tendons on his neck strained.

"Why do you want to know? You're not going to live long enough to do anything about it."

"People were killed when your mole leaked information. I want to know who it was."

"Just try to figure it out." Her smile practically stretched ear to ear. "You men think you're so smart. You think because you have a penis you're so much more clever than us poor, pathetic women."

Jane jumped in, trying to get the attention away from Lex before he exploded. "That's how you've remained undetected for so long. You use women to do your dirty work. James Robert's flock is mostly women, so a few more who work for you wouldn't be noticed. You pick the ones who have been kicked around by men and convince them that this is the way to have their revenge and make money at the same time." Jane had to give Susie credit, she knew how to manipulate people like an expert.

"Very good. You're smarter than I thought. I can spot an abused woman a mile off. Their hunched shoulders give them away every time. James Robert gets them here, then I take over. Pretty soon they're distributing my 'packages' to my dealers and spying on the cops for me. No one would have known there was Meth in Stroudsburg if it wasn't for one little brat who got his hands on his mother's shipment and took off with it."

"The pizza delivery bust. The kid didn't have enough for the cops to trace to a lab because he got it from his mother," Lex said, nodding.

"The thief. I took care of him though. No one messes with me."

"But you still haven't answered my question. Who's the mole at EIS?"

"Wouldn't you like to know?" she taunted.

"Who is the mousiest woman at EIS? Someone who blends in with the woodwork but would have access to valuable information?" Jane asked, watching Susie's face.

"No one but Mac would have the type of information she's talking about. And he'd have it secured on his computer."

"What woman has access to his office?"

"There aren't that many women at EIS. Just Sarah, a few field agents who wouldn't be in a position to get that information, and Alice, his secretary. But she's not a computer hacker. There's no way she could get to those files, they're encrypted."

Susie's smirk told Jane all she needed to know.

"That's it. Alice is your mole."

"But why? I don't get it. She's been at EIS for years."

"Gratitude. Alice was one of my first operatives. I helped her get away from the jerk who used her as a punching bag and then get a job at EIS. In return, she used the information she got from EIS's resources to help me out."

"And Mac never suspected her."

"Why should he? Alice had a clean record, just bad taste in
156

men."

"If she was such a good source of information, why didn't she tell you about EIS investigating Jim Bob?" Lex asked.

"Your boss must have suspected something because he changed his passwords. By the time I got someone to break through again, Sarah had already gotten her paws on my laptop."

"What's going to happen to us?" Jane asked.

Now that her hands were free she might be able to do something, but Susie still held the gun. Granted it wasn't pointing at them anymore but she still had it in her hand. Kickboxing hadn't taught her how to dodge bullets.

"The two of you are going to have a terrible fight. During the lover's quarrel, D'Angelo here is going to shoot you. In dismay at his actions, he'll turn the gun on himself. A tragic case of domestic violence."

"Mac knows I'm here. There'll be an investigation. You'll never get away with it."

"By the time they trace you back to James Robert I'll be long gone."

"And Jim Bob will be left holding the bag. You're more ruthless than I gave you credit for."

"Men always underestimate me." She laid the gun on a box on the floor and tugged out a pair of wire cutters.

Jane didn't think about what to do next, she just acted. Before Susie could stand upright, Jane pushed herself out of the chair and snapped a kick right into Susie's face. Something cracked and Jane was afraid it was one of her toes, but she didn't stop moving.

Susie's head whipped backwards and a spray of blood flew from her nose. Jane grabbed her by the hair and brought her knee up as she smashed Susie's head down. There was another crunch and more blood splattered.

Susie went limp and Jane dropped her to the floor with a thud. Her stomach roiled with nausea when she saw Susie's battered face.

"I thought you were a pacifist?" Lex said when Jane picked up the wire cutters and limped over to him.

"That only works if everyone else is too. Come on, we have to get out of here." She couldn't get the blade of the cutters to fit between the tie and Lex's swollen skin. "This is going to hurt, but I can't get the cutters in."

"Just do it." Lex grunted.

She cut as much skin as she did plastic, but she managed to get him free. "Do you know how to get out? I'm completely lost."

"We'll figure it out. I'm not going to be able to use my hands for a while so you'll have to carry the gun."

"I—I...Okay." She didn't want to touch the awful thing, but if it meant getting them out of here she'd do it.

"Good girl. I wish we had some ties to bind Susie-Q but I don't want to waste the time searching for them. Grab the gun and let's go."

Jane took one last look to make sure Susie was breathing and then followed Lex's orders. She'd gotten good at that.

Chapter Fifteen

Jane opened the door to the storeroom where they'd been held and stepped back so Lex could lead the way. Her sense of direction was so screwed up she had no idea where they were going.

"I don't like the idea of leaving an enemy behind me, but we don't have much choice. How long will she be out?"

"I have no idea. I've never done that on a real person before."

Lex shot her an incredulous look but kept stalking down the hall. "I bet there's an exit near the garage. If we keep heading east we should find it. Once we get there I'll liberate a car and we'll go."

How the heck he knew where east was, Jane had no clue but followed his lead anyway. At least he had a plan.

As they came to a bend in the corridor, Lex held up his hand for her to stop. He inched his head around the corner and jerked it back quickly.

"Quick. Duck into that room there."

Jane fumbled with the handle to the nearest door and prayed it wasn't full of more men like Tank. The room was blessedly deserted. The light from the hallway showed a painfully neat desk and computer. A black bag lay propped against a potted fichus tree.

She picked up the black briefcase with the initials S L B embroidered on the top. "Look. This must be Susie's office," Jane whispered to Lex who stood watch by the door.

"See if you can find anything in there we can use."

"Like her laptop?" Jane unzipped the bag to show the tiny computer.

"Beautiful. Grab it and let's go. I think the coast is clear."

Jane slung the briefcase over her shoulder and followed Lex as he crept silently out of the room.

They worked their way through so many dead ends and twists and turns Jane completely lost her way. If they got separated she'd be up the creek without a paddle.

As if reading her thoughts Lex turned to her. "If we split up, take the computer to Mac. I trust him with my life."

"We're not going to get separated. I don't even know how to get to this Mac person." Just the idea sent rivers of fear flooding through her body. She knew the only way Lex would leave her would be if he were dead.

"I'm just saying, don't try and find me, I'll find you. It's more important to get that information to the authorities. Don't trust anyone but Mac."

He pulled a pen out of his pocket and pushed her shirtsleeve up to expose her wrist. His writing was sloppy since he couldn't grip the pen correctly with his injured hands but she could read the numbers well enough.

"This is Mac's private number, backwards. Find the nearest pay phone and tell him, 'Lex Luther needs Superman.'. He'll know what to do."

"I'm not going anywhere without you," she insisted,

gripping the strap of the briefcase with sweaty palms.

"Shh. I need to think."

They reached the junction of another hallway and Lex appeared to be orienting himself. "This way. I feel a breeze. We must be close to an exit."

Jane didn't feel a breeze but she trusted Lex's judgment. As they scurried up an incline she could detect something other than the strong chemical odor of the lab.

"I smell oil. We must be near the garage."

Lex used both hands to turn the handle to a door at the end of the hall. She caught a glimpse of a huge black car parked in a cavernous garage. They did it.

"Let's go."

Jane scrambled into the car and snapped her seatbelt on over the laptop case. Lex fumbled around under the steering wheel.

Sparks flashed in the dim interior and the car started with a roar. Jane hit the remote on the visor to open the bay door. Lex backed out with a squeal of tires. Several lieutenants stood nearby and jumped out of the way as they pulled out.

Another black-clad man ran out a side entrance of the mission and pointed a huge gun at them. Her heart jumped into her throat as the back window exploded in a mass of splintered glass.

"Get down!" Lex pulled her arm until she lay sprawled over the leather seat.

The seatbelt cut into her waist but she wasn't going to complain. A scream escaped as more glass showered down over her. Lex let out a grunt of pain but Jane couldn't see what had happened to him.

"Hold on, they're trying to close the gates on us."

She felt the muscles of his leg bunch under her cheek as he stomped on the accelerator. There was a screech of metal on metal and a thud, then nothing.

"We made it. You can get up now."

Jane sat up carefully. She was covered in broken glass from the window. Lex had blood dripping down his face from multiple cuts but otherwise appeared safe.

"As soon as we can, we'll ditch this hearse and find a safe location to call Mac." He had to yell over the whistling of the wind coming in through the shattered windows.

She nodded mutely and clutched her arms around her body. Her legs felt weak with leftover fear and adrenaline. Sweat dried on her neck but she was afraid to wipe it off because of the glass shards covering her. She looked out the window at the trees flashing by. Her brain had shut down all logical thought processes. All she had left was a primitive need to cling to Lex and assure herself they were safe.

A glint among the branches caught her attention and she screamed, "Look out!" before pulling on the steering wheel. The car skidded all over the road as Lex fought her for control of the wheel.

Another shot rang out and her window burst into a million pieces. Pain seared her cheek as something hot blazed by her face. Lex let out a cry of pain and slumped to the side. The car began to slow and drift towards the trees lining the road.

"Lex!"

"Take the wheel," he gasped.

Jane reached across and straightened the car out the best she could. Blood pumped slowly from Lex's side.

"Oh my God! You've been shot!"

"Not bad. Just hurts like hell." He clamped his hand over

his wound and tried to take control of the wheel again. Sweat dripped down his frightfully pale face.

"Pull over and I'll drive. I'll keep you safe." She bit her lip to hold back the tears that clogged her throat.

"Can't. Have to keep moving. I'm fine."

Jane turned to check on their pursuers. An SUV crested the rise a little ways back. Far too close for them to pull over.

He might believe the wound wasn't a bad one but the blood kept pumping out and his face was chalk-white. She needed to get him to a hospital and fast. But first she had to make sure Susie's thugs didn't catch them.

"Can you shift over if I move to the back seat? I can hold onto the wheel over the headrest and climb into the driver's seat when you're out of the way. We'll slow down some but we won't stop completely."

He appeared to think about it for a second. They hit a dip in the road and he shuddered. The car swerved alarmingly close to the edge of the cliff as he fought off the pain. "I'll try."

Jane winced when tiny pieces of glass cut into her legs through her jeans as she scrambled into the back seat. It was hard to hold the wheel over Lex, but she managed it with only a few close calls. Thank God, no one was on the other side of the road.

"Climb back over, I've got the wheel," Lex ordered.

His shirt was wet with blood and his hair stuck to the sweat on his neck. How much longer before he went into shock?

The wind whipped her hair into her face when she moved into the front seat. She could barely see through the starred windshield and the two passenger windows were completely blown out. Driving over thirty miles an hour was going to be a treat.

The SUV was fast on their tail.

"Do you think you can lose them?"

"I don't think I have much choice." Jane pressed the gas pedal to the floor and the car shot forward.

Her hands were slippery on the wheel and they tore around curves at speeds no sane person should attempt. Trees buzzed so close to the car Jane swore she could smell leaves. She blew through a stop sign and took a right turn on two wheels.

Cars honked and swerved to the side as she shot through the intersection. The on-ramp for the highway had to be around here somewhere.

A faded sign indicated the entrance was coming up on the left. Jane cut off a battered, red car and almost wiped out a motorcycle when she made the left turn.

"Christ! Susie doesn't have to send anyone after us. Your driving will kill us first."

"Don't complain, they're not on our tail any more, are they?"

"I don't know. I'm afraid to open my eyes."

Jane took a quick glance at him. He didn't look worse than before—which wasn't saying much. She had to find a hospital quickly.

The scenery flew past as she sped down the highway. She searched the passing signs for one with a blue 'H'. They were in the middle of nowhere and street signs were few and far between. With every passing mile, her worry grew.

Lex's breathing had become rapid and she swore she could see a blue tinge to his lips. She passed a tractor-trailer and coughed as the exhaust flooded the interior of their car.

How much longer could they go on like this? The gas gauge was on 'E'. Jane was terrified they'd end up stranded on the side of the road, sitting ducks just waiting for Susie's goons to pick them off. A whimper of fear tried to force its way out of her throat but she fought it back.

This was no time to panic. Lex was counting on her to get them to safety and by God, she was going to do it.

She could do this. There had to be an exit soon. The very next exit she came to she'd find a gas station and call 911 and Lex's friend Mac.

The ding of the low-fuel light coming on made her sweat some more, but she pushed it aside. Lex had either fallen asleep or passed out in the passenger seat. Jane couldn't help but remember the last time she drove while he slept next to her.

They'd been running away from gun-toting men that time too. Lord, she was right back where she started. On the run with no idea where she was headed or what the future would bring.

No, that wasn't true. This time she knew that whatever happened she could handle it. She wouldn't fall apart because there was a disruption in her carefully controlled schedule.

A blue sign appeared on the highway like a gift from God. The next exit was in two miles and, God bless America, there was a hospital near by too.

"I'll take care of you, honey, don't worry," she whispered to Lex.

The hospital was less than a mile from the exit and Jane pulled into the emergency room coasting on fumes. She didn't even make it into a parking space before the engine coughed and died.

"I need a doctor!" she shouted to the security guard who approached her. "Hurry!"

He stopped short at the sight of their bullet-studded car

and jabbered into his walkie-talkie. Jane ran around the car and tried to open the passenger door. It was jammed from the force of several bullets hitting it and she couldn't get it open.

"Here, let me help. You'll hurt yourself." The guard moved her aside.

"I don't care about me! Lex is already hurt. He's been shot! He needs a doctor now." Tears streamed down her face while she yanked at the door.

Several people in hospital scrubs swarmed out of the emergency room doors. One woman with a clipboard stood along side them and another guard helped to open the door.

Lex was buried behind a wall of people as they hauled him onto the stretcher. Shouted orders echoed off the building when they wheeled him towards the doors. Jane ran after them, but the lady with the clipboard stopped her.

"Ma'am, we need some information. Do you give permission for the doctors to treat him?"

"Yes, of course." Jane attempted to slip away but the woman wouldn't let her go.

"What's your relationship to the patient?"

"He's my husband," Jane lied without a pause.

"Do you have insurance?"

"Yes." Why was this woman asking her these inane questions when Lex needed her?

"Do you have your card with you?"

Jane automatically reached for her purse and realized she still carried the laptop. "Ah, no. Can I use your phone? I need to call someone who has that information."

She looked down at the smeared numbers on her wrist and prayed she could get a hold of Mac.

Right about now they could use the real Superman.

Chapter Sixteen

"Is this Mac?" Jane asked when a gruff voice answered the phone with a growled, "Hello."

"Who's asking?"

"My name is Dr. Jane Farmer—"

"How did you get this number?"

"Lex gave it to me—"

"I don't know who you're talking about lady. I don't know anyone named Lex."

Hopelessness swamped her and tears pricked her eyes. She just couldn't handle this on her own. Damn it, Lex told her to call this number if she needed help and boy did she ever need it. Now this guy was saying he didn't even know Lex. What was she supposed to do? Self-pity almost overwhelmed her, but she found a weak spark of self-reliance deep inside her.

She would not give up now. She hadn't dodged bullets and driven like a racecar driver on amphetamines just to have someone who was supposed to be Lex's friend pretend he didn't know him.

"Look, I was given this number and told to say 'Lex Luther needs Superman'. I don't have time to play spy games with someone who's supposed to be a friend of the man lying in an emergency room with a bullet in his side."

Arianna Hart

There was a pause and Jane feared she really did have the wrong number but then the voice came back on the line.

"Dr. Farmer, I apologize. I needed to track this call to make sure someone hadn't gotten this number without Lex's knowledge. We've had some...issues recently." The voice was smooth and cultured now, like melted chocolate instead of sandpaper.

"I know all about your issues. By the way, your secretary is your mole. Now are you going to help me or not?"

"Of course. What can I do?" He didn't seem the least bit fazed by the information that his secretary had betrayed him.

A weight lifted off her shoulders. "First, I need you to give the hospital his insurance information."

"Are you serious?"

"As a heart attack. The dragon lady guarding the door won't let me in to see him until all the paperwork is done. I, ah, told them I was his wife to avoid complications."

"I see. If you give me the fax number there I can send the information over the office line. It's scrambled so it should be secure."

Jane had no idea what he meant or why a fax line had to be secure but she didn't bother to ask. As long as he was taking care of things, his phone line could be sunny-side up and she wouldn't blink twice.

"What else can I do for you?"

"Well, since you're asking. We're going to need transportation out of Pennsylvania, and if someone could take the ministry's laptop off my hands so I don't have to worry about it anymore, I'd be eternally grateful."

"You have the ministry's laptop with you at the hospital?" His cultured voice lost its elegance as he barked out the

168

question.

"What did you want me to do with it?"

"Listen to me. As long as you have that computer you're in danger and so is Lex. Find a secure place and get rid of it. I'll be there as soon as I can, but chances are it'll be a few hours before I can get to Pennsylvania. Stay in the hospital. Do you hear me? Don't leave the safety of the hospital for any reason."

"Okay." The relief she'd felt when he said he'd help faded under a wave of renewed fear.

"Do not go with anyone out of the hospital. When I get there I'll address you as Lois and call myself Clark. Don't go with anyone else. I don't care if they say they're from EIS or the FBI or the right hand of God, don't go with them. Do you understand?"

"Y—yes."

"Any questions?"

The sight of a blue-clad security guard reminded her of something. "Hospitals are required to report all gunshot wounds to the police. What do I tell them when they come to talk to me?"

"I'll deal with the local authorities. Just get rid of that damn computer."

"Great." That was one less thing for her to worry about. Jane opened the door of the room that the secretary had put her in and asked for the fax number. Her head swam and she tried to remember everything Mac said. Her whole world had twisted and turned so much she felt like she was caught in a horror movie and couldn't get out.

After giving Mac the fax number and swearing on her father's grave that she'd stay put, she hung up and went back to the admissions desk. Dragon lady was much happier now that she had an insurance card and billing information and told Jane she could go back and see her husband as soon as she signed the paperwork.

Stabs of pain from the multiple cuts and scrapes she'd gotten from the broken windows hit her as she walked through the heavy double doors out of the waiting room. Various aches prodded her tired body and she wanted nothing more than to collapse onto one of the empty gurneys and sleep for a week.

The only thing that kept her on her feet was fear for Lex. She had to know what was going on with him before she passed out. Her stomach twisted into knots of anxiety when she remembered his pale face and slumped form in the car.

Dear God, please let him be all right.

The smell of antiseptic burned her nose. People bustled efficiently around her and she followed a technician of some sort to Lex's curtained cubicle. A canned voice paged doctors to various floors and a man wearing a hospital johnny announced he was the angel of God come to smite the heathens and disbelievers.

Just another day in the ER. Jane had spent some time during graduate school working in the emergency department and hated every minute of it. The misery and helplessness of the people waiting to hear about the fate of their loved ones was soul-sapping. It took a special kind of person to work in such an environment day after day, and she wasn't too proud to admit she couldn't handle it.

The technician parted the curtain and gestured for Jane to go in. He mumbled something about the doctor needing to ask her some questions, but Jane wasn't paying any attention. Her attention was focused on Lex.

His stubble stood out clearly on his too-pale face. An oxygen mask covered his mouth and nose and hissed quietly in the tiny treatment area. Intravenous lines ran into both his arms and various machines monitored his heart rate and blood pressure.

Jane held her breath and waited for his chest to rise. Relief made her light-headed as she saw the sheet gently lift with his inhalation. He lay so still she'd feared he was already dead.

Someone came in and asked her a million questions. Jane answered them the best she could and lied when she had to. She must have been convincing, because they finally left her alone.

Her heart was in her throat and she clasped Lex's hand. It was limp and clammy, but she didn't care. She could still feel his pulse moving in his wrist and that was all that mattered.

"You're going to be okay," she whispered. "I called Mac and he has everything under control. The doctors here are the best and they'll have you patched up in no time." She didn't have a clue how good the doctors were but she wasn't going to tell Lex that.

Her heart seemed permanently lodged in her throat as she listened to the machines beep. What a fool she'd been to think she could face her fears and remain unscathed. She thought she'd gone about things so intelligently, with her eyes wide open. Now that she had a chance to breathe, she realized she'd justified her desire for Lex by telling herself she was conquering her fears of intimacy.

Instead, she was falling in love with him. And now, he lay clinging to life and she hadn't even had the guts to tell him he meant more to her than a brief affair. Tears leaked down her cheeks and she squeezed his hand even tighter.

"Ma'am? We have your husband's belongings here. We'll need you to sign for them."

Jane wiped her face with the sleeve of her shirt before

facing the security guard. He held a plastic bag with Lex's clothes in it and handed her an itemized sheet for her to sign. She took it blindly and scrawled her name at the bottom.

"Do you want to hold on to his things or would you like us to lock them up until he's in a room?"

The guard's question reminded her that Mac wanted her to get rid of the laptop.

"Could you hold onto them for me? I—I'm not from around here..." She trailed off, and tried to appear as helpless as possible. It didn't take too much acting on her part to pull it off. "Could I just get his wallet so I can have some money for the cafeteria?"

"Sure." He handed her the bag.

The radio at his waist squawked an unintelligible message. He snapped it off his belt and said something back that Jane didn't understand either.

"Ma'am, I need to go. When you're done just give it to the secretary and she'll lock it up for you."

"Thank you." Jane waited as the guard jogged down the hall.

Before anyone else could come in, she dumped Lex's clothes and grabbed his wallet, she really would need some money at some point. Something fell as she pulled the wallet out. A necklace lay on the floor in a pool of silver. She picked it up and glanced at the medal, it said "Saint Christopher, protect us." If ever they needed protection it was right now. She slipped it over her head and tucked it under her shirt.

Having a little piece of Lex with her soothed her frazzled nerves slightly. The cool medal lay heavily against her heart, just like her worry for Lex. Her breath caught on a hiccup of a sob, but she bit it back.

Pull it together, Jane. Everything will be all right. They were in the hospital now. Lex would be safe. And as soon as she got rid of this stupid laptop she'd be safe too.

Her hands shook as she unzipped the briefcase and tugged the small computer out. With a quick glance around her, she stuffed it inside Lex's jeans and folded them up around the laptop. The bag was too small to fit the briefcase as well, so she zipped it up and put it on the floor. The wallet went back in the plastic bag and she sealed it up.

The lady at the desk barely noticed her, other than to have her initial a note stating she took possession of the cash and the medal. If she thought the bag was rather heavy for only having jeans, shoes, some jewelry and a wallet, she didn't say anything.

Jane went back to Lex's room and searched for a doctor. Shouldn't they be doing something besides pumping him full of fluids? The man had a bullet in him for crying out loud. He should have at least a nurse next to him.

"Excuse me?" Jane grabbed a nurse bustling by. "Is there someone here who could tell me what is going on with my husband?"

"The doctor will be with you in just a minute," the harried nurse said as she dragged a cart into another room.

"Another minute" turned out to be a good half hour later. Jane's nerves were worn so thin she was on the verge of creating a scene to end all scenes. By the time the baby-faced doctor pushed his way past the curtain Jane could have ripped his head off.

"Mrs. D'Angelo? I'm Dr. Freedman. Your husband is in serious condition."

No kidding. Did it take a medical degree to figure out a bullet in the side was a "serious condition"?

"X-rays show the bullet is lodged in his pelvis. We don't know what else it may have hit until we bring him in for surgery."

"Then what are you waiting for?" she snapped. She remembered reading that when someone was shot, the bullet didn't just stop once it pierced the skin. Instead it bounced around inside the victim's body doing all sorts of damage.

"He's lost a lot of blood. We need to get his volume up before we risk operating. If we open him up too soon the shock could kill him."

"I'm sorry. I—I'm just so worried."

The thought of Lex dying on the operating table made her stomach drop to her toes. She grabbed his hand and felt for his fluttering pulse. He looked so pale and wan against the white sheets. She couldn't face the idea of him remaining like that for the rest of his life.

"I understand. The good news is I don't believe the bullet hit his spinal cord. He's responding to painful stimuli and his breathing doesn't seem to be compromised. We won't know more until after surgery, but all indications are promising."

"That's good news," She hadn't even considered the bullet could have paralyzed him. Bile rose in her throat.

"It shouldn't be much longer. They're preparing the OR now and Dr. Moore has been paged," the doctor told her as he glanced at his watch.

"Thank you."

If "another minute" was a half hour, how long would "not much longer" be?

The bags of fluid had almost emptied before two orderlies came and disconnected all the machines Lex was plugged into. Jane refused to let go of Lex's hand and so had to practically run along side the gurney as they wheeled it down the crowded hall.

"This is as far as you can go, ma'am. There's a waiting room down the hall. Dr. Moore will get you there when he's out of surgery," one of the large orderlies said when they stopped in a dimly lit corridor in front of a door marked "Authorized personnel only".

Jane nodded, but didn't release Lex's hand. She was terrified that if she let go now she'd never see him again.

"Ma'am, the doctor is waiting."

"Yes, okay." Jane leaned over and kissed Lex's forehead. "You're going to be okay, do you hear me? You're going to be making me crazy again in no time." Tears clogged her voice but she wouldn't let them fall until the stretcher rolled through the doors.

Chapter Seventeen

The clock must be broken. Either that or she was trapped in a time warp. Lex had been in surgery for over an hour, but it seemed like decades had passed. Jane felt sticky from the dried sweat on her back, but didn't want to leave the waiting room to wash up in case the doctor came back with news.

Other family members waited in tense silence for word of their loved ones. The room was filled with so much anxiety Jane felt suffocated by it. An elderly woman dressed in black had a string of rosary beads twined through her gnarled fingers. She rocked slowly in her chair as she mumbled prayer after prayer.

Jane had never been very religious, but right now she welcomed the faint hope that someone would listen to her pleas for Lex's life. She clutched Lex's medal in her fist and begged shamelessly. Intellectually, she knew that her prayers wouldn't change anything, but dumping her worry in someone else's lap for a while brought her a sense of comfort. She'd take what she could get right now.

The coffee she'd consumed had given her a headache and made her stomach roil with nausea. Her muscles ached in places she didn't know she even had muscles and her neck throbbed with tension. Where the hell was Mac? Should she call him again?

A green-clad doctor stood in the doorway and everyone looked up expectantly.

"Mrs. D'Angelo?" he asked.

"Here," Jane said lifting her hand. It felt funny answering to that but she was so worried about Lex she pushed it aside.

"I'm Dr. Moore. Your husband is going to be just fine," he said without fanfare.

"Oh, thank God." Jane sagged back into the chair as her legs refused to hold her weight. Relief made the blood rush in her ears.

"It was touch and go there for a little while. He lost a lot of blood, but we were lucky. The bullet wasn't very powerful by the time it hit him so it didn't do too much soft tissue damage."

Jane stared at him blankly.

"It entered his torso, was deflected downward by a rib, nicked the small intestine and lodged in the pelvic girdle. Rifle wounds tend to do more damage than that after they penetrate, unless most of their velocity has been spent. If there had been more power behind the bullet it could have easily shattered his pelvis and lodged in his spine."

"Dear God." The enormity of the situation almost decimated her, but she held herself together so she could listen to the doctor.

"We're not out of the woods yet. There's still the risk of infection or a secondary injury, but overall I feel optimistic he'll make a complete recovery."

"When can I see him?"

"He's in recovery now. You can take a quick look at him, but you won't be able to stay. I'm keeping him heavily sedated for the next twelve hours. From here he'll go to the Critical Care Unit. A nurse will let you know when they have a bed for him on the unit."

"Thank you." She followed Dr. Moore to the recovery room.

"He's going to be groggy. We don't want him to come out of sedation too suddenly and rip out his breathing tube or drains. He probably won't even know you're there, so don't be alarmed if he doesn't respond to you."

Jane said nothing as he parted the curtain and motioned for her to go in. She didn't even recognize Lex under all the tubes and wires. He moaned softly around a tube that was stuck down his throat and a nurse injected something into his IV line.

There was no place for Jane to touch him. She couldn't hold his hand because he had something clipped to his finger and an IV in the back of his hand. One of the monitors showed a wavy line slowly bouncing up and down. Jane took comfort in watching his heart beat steadily.

"He'll be here for a while if you'd like to get something to eat," the nurse said helpfully as she adjusted one of the tubes going down to a bag on the side of the bed. "I'll get you the minute he wakes up, I promise."

"Thank you." The last thing she felt like doing was eating right now, but she couldn't stay here.

Bending down, she kissed Lex lightly on the forehead. "I'll be here when you wake up. You rest and get stronger," she whispered.

Jane followed the signs until she got back to the waiting room. She took one glance at all the tense faces in there and knew she couldn't spend another minute in there. Even if she wasn't hungry, she should probably try to choke down something to eat. Maybe she could find a place to wash up too. She'd cleaned her hands and face in the waiting room lav, but it would take a real shower to get all the shards of glass out of her hair.

Hopefully, by the time she was done Mac would be there. It would be nice to have someone else around who was as worried about Lex as she was.

Jane left word with the receptionist in the waiting room that she'd be in the cafeteria in case Lex woke up while she was gone. The woman made a note of Lex's name and doctor and assured Jane she'd find her if anything changed. She handed her the laptop case that she'd held onto while Jane was with Lex and went back to her crossword puzzle.

The case was empty except for some power cords, but Jane didn't get rid of it. When this was all over they might need those cords to get the information off the laptop. Besides, it might seem a little suspicious if she threw it in the nearest garbage can.

The cafeteria was almost deserted which suited Jane just fine. She didn't want to fight for a seat or have to talk to anyone. Even though her appetite was non-existent, she bought a bowl of soup and a bottle of ice water. Maybe the watery chicken noodle would settle her stomach a bit.

Her sense of time was completely thrown off. She spied a large clock on the wall and was surprised to see it was only four in the afternoon. How long had she been here? What time had she called Mac? It felt like she'd been at the hospital for days but really it had only been a couple hours.

She'd had more adventure in the last twenty-four hours than in her entire thirty-three years. Of course, that wasn't saying much. Her life up to this point hadn't been that exciting.

Steam wafted up from the spoonful of soup and Jane thought about her life before this week. It was like watching a black and white movie. A boring, black and white movie. With the sound off.

Nothing like living on the edge to add a little color to one's life. She could never go back to her washed out, emotionless world again. Once the genie was out of the bottle there was no stuffing it back in. She'd found strength she'd never known she possessed, and she wouldn't get rid of it even if she could.

This week had changed her, and no matter what happened in the future between her and Lex, she couldn't regret the change. That is, if Lex lived through it.

"Dr. Farmer?" A man in a pinstriped suit stopped at her table.

"Yes? Did Lex wake up?" She scrambled out of her chair and slipped the laptop case over her shoulder, ready to go to the recovery room.

"I don't know. I haven't been there yet. I'm Don from EIS." He stuck out his hand for her to shake.

Jane took it automatically but warning bells went off in her head. "Isn't Mac coming?" she asked, pulling her hand away.

"There was a complication and he sent me instead. Something about the police station and Alice. He told me to come down here and get you and the evidence to a safe house until he could get free."

Danger! More bells blared.

She hadn't seen this particular man at the compound before, but that didn't mean he wasn't one of Susie's thugs. Jane scanned the cafeteria and realized she was almost totally alone except for a woman counting money at the register.

What would Lex do? He sure as hell wouldn't be sitting here wringing his hands, he'd ask for ID.

"I'm sorry if this sounds terribly rude, but could I see some ID?"

"EIS agents don't carry IDs. We're private contractors, not

federal agents."

What now?

"Okay, well I'm sure you won't mind if I call Mac and confirm he sent you."

"I told you, he's at the police station. He doesn't have time to mess around. We need to get you and that laptop to safety before the Great Hope Ministry comes after you."

Nerves made her hands shake. She'd thought this whole mess had ended when they escaped from the ministry, but she wasn't willing to trust anyone yet. Mac had given her very specific instructions when she'd spoken to him. If he really did have an emergency of some sort he'd have called the hospital. She wasn't naïve enough to fall for this guy's act.

"I'm not going anywhere until I hear from Mac." Jane searched for a weapon but all she had was her plastic spoon and cardboard container of soup.

Steaming hot soup.

"Lady, you're coming with me." He reached for her arm.

Before he could get a grip on her, Jane grabbed her bowl of soup and threw it in his face. He screamed in agony as scorching noodles clung to his cheeks. Jane lashed out at his knee with the heel of her sneaker-clad foot. Don—or whatever his name was—stumbled and she gave him a little extra push for good measure.

As he fell, he reached out for her leg. Fear made the adrenaline pump in her veins and Jane jumped over him and ran for the door.

The cafeteria was on the ground floor, all she had to do was find the nearest door and she'd be free. She dared a look over her shoulder and saw Don limping his way through the empty cafeteria towards her. He barked orders into a cell phone.

If he was talking to someone on a cell phone, he obviously wasn't alone. Brilliant deduction, Doctor. Instead of going outside, Jane ran for the stairway and bolted up the stairs.

The last thing she wanted was to be trapped outside away from any security guards. Her heart leapt into her throat as her foot slipped on one of the treads and she crashed to one knee on the hard cement.

Get up! Keep moving or die! A voice amazingly like Lex's pushed her on.

She lost count of how many flights she'd gone up when she heard the door below her slam open. Don had found her.

"We've got this place surrounded, bitch. You might as well give up now."

"Bite me," she murmured to herself. She wouldn't waste the energy it took to shout it at him. Besides, that would only pinpoint her location and she really didn't want to give him any more help than absolutely necessary.

A red sign said "3" but what the heck was on the third floor? She pushed open the door and saw a mural of angels and storks.

Must be the maternity ward. She couldn't lead this lunatic in there with all the babies. He could very well have a gun on him. She wouldn't take that chance.

Jane let the door close behind her and flew up the next flight of stairs. Where was the psych ward? The psychiatric unit always had lots of nice, big, burly orderlies. If she could find that floor she'd be safe. Or safer, anyway.

Her mind ran as fast as her legs while she tried to remember if she'd seen a map or directory. She'd been so worried about Lex that she hadn't thought about taking a tour of the hospital.

Think! She could hear Don climbing the stairs behind her, his longer legs making up for her head start. Guess she didn't kick him as hard as she thought. Next time she'd go for his toes. He wouldn't be gaining on her if he had two broken toes on his foot.

Next time? Was she insane? There would be no next time.

Her knee throbbed and her hands stung from her earlier fall but she kept going. How many floors did this place have anyway? A red sign said "Roof" with an arrow pointing upwards.

Well, that answered that question. She had to take this door or she'd end up on the roof. Getting into a wrestling match with someone Don's size on the roof was not a good scenario.

Jane ripped through the last door, determined to find a security guard or orderly or even a janitor to help her. The sight of a glassed-in admissions desk and thick doors was the most beautiful thing she'd ever seen. Chances were this wasn't Hospice.

"Please! Help me." Jane begged the woman sitting behind a thick wall of unbreakable glass. "Someone is after me. He may be armed."

The woman looked up and her eyes widened. She punched a button and alarms went off all over the place.

Oh great, she thought Jane was an escaped patient.

"I'm not crazy, someone really is after me. Please, let me in."

The intercom blared overhead, "Dr. Strong to North Seven. Dr. Strong to North Seven."

Jane knew from her internship that that message wasn't paging a real doctor. It was a call to get security up here without panicking the hospital. Fine, she'd let them take her into a padded room if it meant she was safe from Donny-boy.

But would they get here in time?

The thunder of the stairwell door hitting the wall echoed down the hall. Don had won the race.

Jane ran to the doors to the ward and yanked on them hopelessly. There was nothing to hide behind up here, no chairs or plants or anything in the hallway. If Don had a gun she'd be a sitting duck.

"What're you going to do now?" Don asked while he stalked her. "There's no way out of here, everything is locked tight. It's just me and you."

"I'm not going with you. If you try to take me out of here someone will call the police. Security is already on their way." She shot a look over her shoulder and saw the woman who'd been behind the desk had fled. Jane was on her own.

He didn't reach for a gun. That was a good sign. Okay, so he was twice her size, she only had to hold on until security arrived. She could do that, right?

Damn right she could. Resolution straightened her spine and the shaking in her knees stopped. She was still scared spitless, but she could survive.

The first thing she needed to do was not let him corner her next to the door. Her only chance at staying alive was to stay out of his reach. Even if she had more than the basics of self-defense, he was still much bigger than her and she'd lost the element of surprise with her kick in the cafeteria.

Keep him off balance.

"What rock did Susie find you under? I thought she normally used women for her dirty work." She slid away from the door, but stayed close to the desk. There was probably a camera there. If she couldn't hold Don off and he did grab her, at least he'd be caught on film.

Great. She'd be dead but at least Mac would know who did it.

"Susie only uses women as snitches and mules. She uses men for the real work."

"Oh really? Seems to me she doesn't much care for men. You're nothing more than an errand boy." She had years of study in the human mind. It was about time she put them to use.

"Give it up. I'm not going to turn on my boss just because you're throwing insults around."

He held his hands wide and came towards her slowly. At least he wasn't trying to rush her. He must still be smarting from the soup and the kick. Good.

"You have a chunk of carrot in your hair." She crouched into a fighting stance and held her hands up in a guard position. If she survived this she was going to sign up for karate.

He growled low and came at her. Jane lashed her foot out at his sore knee but he blocked it. Pain smashed into her toes from the force of his block. She managed to bring her foot back before he latched onto it, but only just barely in time.

"Try again, sweetie. I'm wise to your tricks now."

Oh goody. Where the hell was security? If she'd really been an escaped patient she'd have been long gone by now.

Don reached for her again, and she twisted out of the way. Right into the elbow he rammed into her mid-section. Air whooshed out of her lungs and half the contents of her stomach came up her esophagus.

He yanked her arms behind her while she retched helplessly. Oh God, she was going to die and there was nothing she could do about it.

Choking back another heave, she raked the sole of her shoe down Don's shin and jerked her head back as hard as she could.

Right into his nose. Blood spattered everywhere but he still didn't let go. What else could she do? Her head rang with the impact of hitting his face, her stomach hurt so badly she couldn't stand up straight, how could she get out of here?

The toes! Break the toes. Desperation put extra muscle in her strike and she stomped hard on his loafer-clad foot. Something crunched under her heel as she slammed it down a second time.

Don let out an agonized scream and released her. Jane stumbled forward and fell to her knees. She kept moving anyway. She'd crawl down seven flights of stairs if that's what it took to get her out of here.

Strong hands grabbed her and lifted her up. Jane screamed and struggled against them until she felt a needle jab her in the butt. She lifted her head to see several security guards and men in scrubs rushing through the locked doors of the ward.

She saw two men holding a bleeding, moaning Don while a security guard snapped handcuffs on his wrists. Relief rushed through her as her world went gray.

Chapter Eighteen

Jane swam through a mist. She could hear voices and beeps but they didn't make any sense in her fuzzy state so she ignored them. Dream figures shifted and moved through the fog in her head.

James Robert stood behind a mile-high pulpit and brought down fire with his words. Susie's head was atop a bloated spider's body and she scuttled over an enormous web that held the bodies of beaten-down men and women.

She moaned and tried to run away from the images but they kept coming at her. Where was Lex? What happened to Lex? She could hear his voice in the fog but couldn't find him. Was he dead? Had she killed him? Accusing voices surrounded her, dismembered fingers pointed at her, pushing her deeper into the darkness until she succumbed and dreamed no more.

Later, much later, she fought through the mist again. This time she managed to crack her eyes open slightly. Her vision was blurry so she blinked a few times until it cleared.

"Good morning, Lois. I'm Clark." A tall, sandy haired man with the bluest eyes she'd ever seen loomed over her.

She tried to pull back but her arms were bound to the bed.

"Restraints?" she croaked. Her voice was raspy and her head throbbed with confusion. Where was she, and why was she tied down?

"A precaution I couldn't talk them out of. Apparently you made quite an impression on the staff and they weren't taking any chances."

This must be Mac. Her fuzzy brain struggled to remember the events that led to her getting strapped down on a hospital bed. She had spoken to him on the phone. He'd told her not to go with anyone who didn't give her the code words.

The cafeteria. Someone had tried to say they were from EIS and she'd run away.

"How long have I been sedated? How's Lex? What happened to Don?"

"I've been here for several hours. When I got here you were already sedated, so I'd say you've been out of it for a good six to eight hours. Lex has been moved to a room and is also sleeping. No one knows a goddamn thing about why you were fighting with a man twice your size or who the hell he is." He ran a hand through his hair and collapsed in the plastic chair by her bed.

"He told me you sent him, but he didn't have the code words. I threw soup at him and ran up the stairs." She closed her eyes to try and remember better but it made her head spin so she opened them again.

"Smart move. I take it he didn't get the laptop then? The case is empty."

"I hid it in Lex's pants and had security lock them up for me."

Mac let out a sigh of relief.

"I tried to explain to the doctors that you weren't a threat to yourself or others but after looking at the man you beat up they didn't believe me. Now that you're awake and I know more of the story I can smooth things over and get you released."

"What happened to Susie? And James Robert?" If she had

been unconscious for hours Susie could have easily gotten away.

"Someone at the ministry heard the gunshots and alerted the police. The chief of police had had the compound under observation for a while so he had units in place. He's holding them for questioning for twenty-four hours."

"Why hasn't he arrested them? They killed Sarah and tried to kill us. Susie has been shipping drugs all over the country. And James Robert is conning people out of all their money and gambling it away." Her throat felt like she'd gargled with razor blades, but she had to let Mac know what a threat Susie was. "They should be locked up forever for all they've done."

"Ah, yes, but the chief doesn't know any of that. All he knows is the compound is in shambles, and shots were fired. Until he has reasonable cause, he can't charge them with anything. Which is why that laptop is so important, as is your testimony and Lex's."

"So she doesn't just want the laptop, she wants me dead." Jane struggled against the leather bonds that held her. "Get these things off me. I'm a sitting duck here."

"Relax. I told you, she's in police custody." He laid a placating hand on her arm.

"You don't understand. She has people at the police station. She has people everywhere, that's why she hasn't been caught yet."

Mac didn't waste time arguing with her. He pulled a tiny phone off his belt and began issuing orders like a field general. "I'll get a doctor in here immediately." He stormed out the door.

Jane's head spun dizzily as she struggled to break free of the leather restraints. It was impossible. They made these suckers strong enough to hold dangerously mentally ill patients. She wasn't going to get out of them without losing a limb.

God, she prayed Susie didn't have someone at the police station with enough authority to break her out of there. Lord only knew how many people she had at her beck and call. If what Susie had said at the compound was true, her web spread over the whole country.

The image of Susie as a spider flashed into her head when she remembered her drug-induced dream. Dream, ha, more like a nightmare. This whole day had been a nightmare.

A nurse walked into the room and Jane turned her head expectantly. Mac must have gotten the doctor to place the order to remove the bonds already. Boy, he worked fast.

"Are you here to take these off?" Jane asked.

The nurse stood by the door without moving. Jane didn't want to antagonize her, but she really wanted the restraints off.

"Not exactly." The nurse opened the door a crack and peered out. She crossed to the corner of the room and pushed a button on a box attached to the ceiling.

Jane hadn't noticed the box before. What was the woman doing? Fresh alarm bells rang through Jane's muddled head. The nurse was acting really weird and her behavior sent panic streaking through Jane's system.

"What are you doing?" Jane cried as the "nurse" crossed the room to the bed and pulled a syringe out of her pocket.

"Susie sends her regards," the nurse replied and she squirted fluid through the needle.

"Mac! Security! Help!" Jane screamed at the top of her lungs.

"Shut up!" the nurse snarled.

She clamped a hand over Jane's mouth and tried to line up the needle on Jane's arm at the same time.

Jane bit down hard on the hand over her mouth and tasted blood. She kicked her legs, which were thankfully unbound, and thrashed her head from side-to-side.

When the nurse's hand fell away from her face she screamed again. "Mac! Security!" She twisted her shoulders as much as possible to keep the needle out of her arm. The nurse couldn't hold her down and stab her at the same time.

"Help! Help!"

No one was going to hear her through the thick doors. And even if they did, the staff here was used to hysterical screams, they wouldn't think anything of it.

The nurse threw her body across Jane's chest to subdue her. Jane could smell stale smoke in the woman's hair and almost gagged. She brought her knees up as hard as she could in her weakened state and managed to connect with the nurse's hip. It wasn't a very effective hit but it stopped the needle from going into her arm.

"Go ahead and fight. It'll make it work that much faster when I finally stick you," she grunted, moving higher up away from Jane's knees.

The nurse's weight settled on Jane's chest, cutting off her ability to breathe. Her shoulder jammed into Jane's collarbone and Jane feared it would snap under the pressure.

With the last of her strength, Jane smashed her head forward, right into the nurse's forehead. Pain exploded through her brain and stars danced across her vision.

The nurse collapsed on top of her. Her dead weight crushed Jane's ribcage, and she couldn't breathe. Spots swam in front of her eyes as she gasped for oxygen.

Jane tried to scream but couldn't so much as whisper. She thrashed from side-to-side but couldn't dislodge the nurse's body.

Oh God, she'd managed to keep from being poisoned, but now she was going to suffocate. Either way she was dead. Jane shoved her feet under her and arched her hips, hoping to move the nurse a few critical inches so she could breathe.

The bedrail held the nurse's lower body and kept her from falling one way or the other. Jane's head swam and her vision grayed as she bucked her hips up. It wasn't doing much good, but if she stopped she'd be dead for sure.

Another heave caused the nurse's head to flop lower on Jane's chest. A tiny bit of air seeped into her lungs and she gulped like a drowning swimmer. The oxygen gave her strength and she thrashed harder, pushing her hips high and then dropping them down suddenly. Her wrists burned from stretching the bonds as far as they would go, but she refused to stop trying.

The nurse slid another inch and Jane fought harder. Finally, gravity kicked in and the nurse fell to the floor. Jane's lungs expanded and she drew in great big gulps of air.

Her head throbbed mercilessly, her body felt bruised and battered and she was afraid her collarbone might be fractured, but she was alive.

"What's going on here? Why is your video monitor turned off?" A muscle-bound man wearing white scrubs came into the room and stopped short when he saw the body of the nurse on the floor.

Jane forgot that all psych rooms had video surveillance. So that's what the fake nurse had been doing. She must have shut off the camera when she came in.

The orderly opened the door wide and shouted for security. Mac charged in, cell phone still to his ear, as several more orderlies piled into the room. A man wearing a white lab coat ran in behind them.

Leap of Faith

"Who is this? What happened? Why is she still bound?" Mac shouted questions to the room in general.

Everyone began speaking at once, and the cacophony was deafening. The doctor let out a sharp whistle that pierced Jane's skull like a knife, but quieted the room down.

"Now, will someone please explain what's going on here?" the doctor asked.

"I came to check the video camera because the monitor had gone black. When I got here I found this woman on the floor," the orderly said, shifting his feet from side-to-side.

"Does anyone know who this woman is or why she's lying unconscious on the floor?"

Someone bent down and looked at the ID tag flipped face down on her shirt. "It's a fake. See, there's no hospital logo when you tip it to the light."

"She came in and turned off the camera, then tried to stab me with a needle." Jane didn't repeat the "Susie sends her regards" part of the story. She didn't think Mac wanted to air all the dirty laundry just yet.

"You—" The doctor pointed to the nearest orderly, "—take the restraints off." The man jumped to obey. "You and you, take this person to another room and hold her there. I want to find out how an imposter managed to get into a locked ward."

People scrambled all over themselves to obey the doctor and soon Jane's arms were free and the fake nurse removed from the room. She hurt all over as she tried to sit up, but she didn't stop moving. The sheer freedom to scratch her nose was almost intoxicating.

"Mr. McLean, I don't know what's going on around here, but if someone has sabotaged my floor I want to know about it."

"I'll be sure to fill you in completely once I find out what's

193

happening," Mac replied. "Is my associate free to go?"

The doctor eyed Jane and grunted. "She looks like she could use a few more hours in bed but she doesn't belong in the psych ward. Maybe the CCU, but not the ward."

The Critical Care Unit. That's where Lex was. If they sent someone for her that meant they could send someone after him too.

"Lex!" Jane shouted and pushed off the bed.

Her bare feet hit the floor and her legs barely supported her weight. "They could be after Lex."

A cool breeze blew across her back, and Jane realized she was naked except for a thin hospital gown. She didn't care. She had to get to Lex before someone poisoned him.

"Call the CCU and warn them not to let anyone into Luther D'Angelo's room," Mac ordered the doctor as he shoved ahead of Jane.

He flew down the hall far quicker than she could move. She only hoped it was quickly enough. Grabbing a bathrobe off a laundry cart, she shuffled her way to the elevator. Several members of the hospital staff gave her bemused stares as she wrestled the robe on, but no one stopped her.

Jane made it out of the locked ward and into the hall in time to see the stairway door close. Her legs ached just thinking about climbing down several flights of stairs barefoot. She'd done it once and hadn't really enjoyed the experience.

The elevator door dinged at that moment and Jane took it as a sign she shouldn't try to follow Mac on the stairs. She waited until two chatting nurses got out of the elevator and ambled up the hall before she ran for the rapidly closing doors.

Please don't look over and try to stop the escaped patient. Jane could only imagine how bad she appeared after the beatings she'd taken today.

She squeezed inside the elevator before the doors closed all the way and punched the button for the CCU. Pressing the "close doors" button repeatedly—like that would make them close faster—she held her breath until the car lurched downward.

Please God, let Mac be in time.

Chapter Nineteen

Jane shuffled into the CCU and searched for Lex's room. A tray of wicked-looking metal implements lay on the floor and several laundry carts were scattered across the hall. She followed the mess until she spotted a cluster of blue-clad security guards.

Hmm, was this Lex's room?

They'd caused more confusion and excitement at St. Mary's hospital in the few hours they'd been there than it had probably seen in months. A petite woman wearing scrubs lay face down on the floor while a security guard cuffed her hands behind her back.

Had Mac stopped her in time? Jane searched the room frantically until she saw Mac slumped in a chair being tended to by a stunning blonde. Where was Lex?

Jane pushed her way into the crowded room. Machines and wires and tubes surrounded the bed. There were too many people for her to see if Lex was part of the lumpy mess on the bed. She wiggled and wormed her way through the crowd until she managed to get further into the room.

Lex's scratchy face peering at her blearily was the most beautiful thing she'd ever seen.

"Hey, Doc, come to share the excitement?" His voice was husky and slightly slurred, but it sounded wonderful to her.

"Yeah, I was getting bored on the psych ward." She couldn't stop herself from kissing his forehead and clutching his hand in hers.

He looked pale and sickly, but he was alive.

"The psych ward? Were you working?"

"No, I was a patient. It's a long story," she said at his confusion. "I'll tell you about it when I'm sure you'll be able to stay awake. I take it Mac got here in time to stop Susie's latest flunky."

"Yup. I don't really know what happened. I'm so drugged up I don't know what's real and what's a dream."

"When you're better we'll go through everything, I promise." She pressed another kiss to his stubbled cheek.

"Are you okay? You've got bruises all over your face."

"You should see the other guy," she said, turning her head away. "Like I said, it's a long story. I'm just glad you're safe."

"Me too. Will you stay here?" His eyes began to drift close but he blinked them open again.

"You couldn't tear me away. Sleep. I'll be here when you wake up."

"Need to talk to you. Important," he muttered before drifting off into a drug-induced slumber.

Jane stroked the unruly hair off his forehead and readjusted the oxygen tube under his nose. She wasn't leaving him alone again without a fight.

The security guards hauled the struggling woman out of the room and the crowd of onlookers slowly drifted away. The blonde nurse straightened and peeled off her gloves. She shot a sultry look at Mac before she left.

His face remained expressionless, but Jane was sure she saw a glint of appreciation in his eyes. Hmmm, wasn't that interesting.

"Are you okay?" Jane asked Mac once the room cleared.

"Just a tiny cut over my eye. It's nothing."

"What happened?" She kept her voice low so as not to wake Lex.

Mac pulled up a chair for her and brought in another one from the hallway.

"When I got here, that woman had a syringe already in Lex's IV line. I dove at her and dislodged it. End of story."

"What was in the syringe? Did she inject any of it in his line?" Jane jumped up and scrutinized the clear plastic tubes as if she could see the poison and stop it.

"The syringe had strychnine in it, and yes, I managed to stop her in time. If even a little had gotten into him he'd be dead already. They pulled the line just in case, so you can stop staring. That's the secondary line you're about to yank out of his arm."

Jane dropped the tube and sat back down. Her hands shook as she thought about how close Lex had come to an agonizingly painful death.

"If you're okay here, I'm going to make some phone calls. I want to make sure Susie doesn't get out on bail. That's one dangerous woman, and no one knew it but you."

"I'm a psychologist. Believe it or not, I can read people pretty well. Usually. Although I didn't realize what she was up to until it was almost too late." Jane shook her head, mad at herself.

She'd had a bad feeling about Susie the moment she met her, but she hadn't realized the depth of Susie's depravity.

"Susie confounded several drug enforcement and federal agencies for months. Cut yourself some slack."

"Thanks. I guess it just goes to show I'm not cut out for this spy business."

"We're consultants, not spies. And from where I'm standing, you did a damn good job. You successfully went undercover with little training or backup and got your partner to safety. With some real training you'd make a great EIS employee."

"Are you offering me a job?" Jane gaped at him in shock. "I don't think your company has much call for an out-of-work marriage therapist," she said.

Mac tapped his chin. "I don't know about that. With your training and insight you could be a valuable asset to our teams in the field. It's something to think about."

Yeah, right. Jane didn't say anything but she was almost certain Mac was only trying to make her feel better. She'd botched this thing up at every turn. There was no way he'd want her anywhere near a case his company was working on ever again.

"I'll be back after I make some calls. Do you have anything to change into? I believe they cut your clothes off after they sedated you."

Oh great. She'd gone from tailored suits to tight jeans to a hospital gown. "No, I'm afraid our clothes are still at the campsite."

"I'll arrange to have some clothes delivered then."

"Lex will need some too. They cut off his shirt in the emergency room."

He made a note on his handheld computer and nodded. "I'll see to it. Make sure you eat something. You've had a busy day and your body will need refueling."

"Yes, sir." She gave him a mock salute.

A half-smile turned up the corners of his mouth as he stood and walked out of the room.

Jane wiggled a bit on the seat and tried to make herself more comfortable. All the abuse her body had taken in the last twenty-four hours crashed down on her. She ached down to her very marrow.

Thank God, this was over. Lex wasn't out of the woods yet, but he seemed to be healing. She'd make sure nothing else happened to interrupt that healing.

Yup, her grand adventure was winding to a close. Pretty soon she'd go back to her condo and start hunting for a job. She'd have her quiet, normal life back.

Sure, she'd see Lex, when he was in-between assignments. Maybe they'd even date or something. Her heart lurched at the thought of never touching him again.

Could she go back to being his distant neighbor after becoming so close to him? What if he brought some other woman home some night? It wasn't like they'd made any commitments to each other.

Lord, she couldn't handle that. Jane gazed at his sleeping face and felt her heart flip over in her chest. She'd only just realized she loved him. She couldn't bear the thought of letting him go now.

A lady never chases a man. She lets him come to her.

Oh for the love of little green apples. Who gave a damn about what a lady should do? A woman would go after what she wanted and not give up.

If she wanted a relationship with him, or even the chance to find out if there was something special between them, by God, she'd go after it. She wasn't going to sit by like some tragic gothic heroine and pine for him.

And with the fires of determination burning inside her, Jane curled into a ball on the chair and fell asleep still holding Lex's hand.

ℰℭ

A rush of cool air over his groin—his naked groin—woke Lex from his pain-filled daze. He unglued his eyelids and saw a blonde in scrubs poking at his stomach. She glanced over at him when she noticed he was awake.

"Are you in a lot of pain, Mr. D'Angelo?"

He felt like he'd been hit by truck. Hell yeah he was in a lot of pain, but he didn't like being out of control so he shook his head. "Nothing I can't handle."

His throat felt raw and raspy from the breathing tube. The nurse noticed and swabbed his mouth with a damp sponge.

"I'm afraid you can't have any liquids for another twelve hours."

Lex grunted, he knew the drill.

A soft breath of air brushed over his hand, and he spotted Jane's upper body sprawled on the edge of the bed. That just couldn't be comfortable, but he wasn't about to wake her up and ask her to move.

Seeing her safe next to him eased the fist that had tightened unknowingly around his heart. He didn't know what had happened to her while he'd be under the knife, but it couldn't have been good. She was covered in bruises and cuts. It killed him to know she'd been fighting for her life while he'd been unconscious.

"Would you like me to have your wife moved to a spare bed?" the nurse asked as she finished marking something down on his chart.

"I don't want to wake her. Could you put a blanket over her?" His wife? Jane had some explaining to do. Although, he had to admit, he liked the sound of that.

"Of course."

She slipped out of the room and returned a few seconds later with a thick blanket. As soon as it was laid over Jane, she snuggled into it and curled up in the chair.

"Thank you. She looks much more comfortable now."

"Sure." The nurse didn't seem to think so, but Lex didn't care.

When he was alone again he let his eyes roam over Jane. He couldn't stop looking at her. How close had he been to losing her?

Too close.

Hell, he could still lose her. They hadn't really discussed their future together. Not that that was such a surprise. With everything happening so fast they hadn't known if they'd see the next sunrise. Now they'd have plenty of time to talk about what came next.

And that scared him a hell of a lot more than Susie's goons did.

What if Jane didn't want to keep seeing him after this? What if once they went back to Connecticut she froze him out like before? In the past, on the rare occasion the woman he was with ended things first, he just moved on. Maybe his ego was a little bruised, but his heart remained untouched.

The idea that Jane might give him the brush-off sent a cold chill down his spine. There was no way he was letting that happen. Sure, it might take some convincing on his part, but he wasn't letting Jane walk away without a fight.

He knew there was more between them than just adrenaline-fuelled sex. The question was, how could he prove that to her? He didn't think she still thought of him as a playboy. At least not seriously. But did she consider him husband material?

Lord, after that last jerk she married, would she even consider getting married again? He was nothing like that cheating bastard, but she didn't necessarily know that.

Crap, crap, crap.

His heart had never ached like this at the thought of losing someone before. Like a piece of his soul would wither away if she left.

How had this happened? He'd always considered himself immune to falling in love. Apparently not, because if this wasn't love he'd eat his shirt.

Of course, he didn't have a shirt right now, but that wasn't the point. His eyes drifted closed and he didn't bother to fight the slumber dragging him down. Tomorrow he'd find a way to make Jane realize he was the best thing that had ever happened to her.

Even if he did almost get her killed.

ଶେଓଃ

The racket of several female voices raised in argument woke Jane from a dead sleep. Someone had put a warm blanket over her and dimmed the lights in the room. What time was it? She rubbed her eyes groggily and read the clock on the wall.

Seven o'clock? But a.m. or p.m.? And what day? Everything was so confused she had no idea how long she'd been in the hospital. Her neck ached something fierce and every muscle in her body throbbed in pain. The spot on her forehead where she'd head-butted the fake nurse pulsed in agony.

Maybe the nurses could give her some of Lex's pain meds? She saw he still slept soundly and sighed in envy.

"I'm his mother! I don't care who's with him, I'm going in!" a voice echoed through the halls.

Other equally loud voices chimed in. Jane couldn't make out the words in the confusion of shouts. She was sure she heard Italian mixed in with prayers and swears.

A sick feeling twisted in her gut. Didn't Lex say he had a bunch of sisters living in New York? New York wasn't that far from Pennsylvania. In fact, it was quite close.

Oh no. That couldn't be Lex's family out there. Please God, don't let that be his mother shouting down the place wanting to get in.

Jane smoothed down the front of her hospital gown and ran her fingers through her hair. It was matted with sweat and probably blood and was in desperate need of a wash. She couldn't meet Lex's family like this. She wasn't even wearing underwear.

Before she could find a place to hide, a tiny, rotund woman pushed open the curtain to Lex's room. Four mirror images ranging in age from mid-forties to early thirties stood behind her.

All five of them glared at Jane with dark eyes the exact same shade as Lex's.

"This, this woman, she tells me you're my son's wife?" Her voice was low and thick with an Italian accent. "I tell her, no that cannot be. My Luther is not married. He would never break his momma's heart by getting married and not telling me."

Jane's palms began to sweat and she stood up as straight as her aching body would let her.

"Mrs. D'Angelo, please let me explain," Jane began in a conciliatory voice. Even though she stood a good six inches over the tallest of them, fear snaked down her spine. "I was on assignment with Lex—er, Luther—and as part of our cover we pretended to be married. When we arrived at the hospital there was still a risk of discovery so we kept up the charade. There hasn't been a chance to straighten things out yet."

Not exactly the truth but it would work for now. Where the hell was Mac? He should be here talking to Lex's family, not her. And where were the clothes he'd promised to get?

Mrs. D'Angelo's eyes zeroed in on her hand holding Lex's. She raised one salt-and-pepper eyebrow at her and folded her arms over her impressive chest. "That looks a little more convincing than a cover." Her mirror images nodded like one.

Jane dropped his hand like it burned her. "Lex and I are neighbors too. We've become very close recently. I'll just get out of the way so you can visit with your son."

Jane moved away from the bed so the D'Angelo women could flock around their fallen member and shuffled out of the room as fast as she could. As she fled the scene, she heard a babble of Italian whispers and knew they were talking about her. Great. What a way to make a first impression. One of the nurses at the station tossed Jane a sympathetic glance as she fled.

She should save her sympathies for herself. Those women were going to drive the nurses nuts by the end of the day. But Lex would be better protected than if the entire police force guarded him. That thought made her feel a little better.

Sun shone through a wide window so Jane deduced it was seven a.m. She'd slept through most of the last day in one way or another.

What had happened to Mac though? He'd gone to make

some phone calls and she hadn't seen him since. She couldn't very well go searching the streets for him dressed in a thin johnny and hospital robe. She'd just have to wait for him in the family lounge and hope he returned with some clothes quickly.

Mac, the rat, was sitting on a sofa in the family waiting area. He had a laptop plugged in and several disposable coffee cups were spread out around him.

"Working hard?" Jane asked from the doorway. The room was empty, thank God.

"Jane. You're awake." He looked at her rather sheepishly and she knew he was the one who called Lex's family.

"You could have given me some warning before you let Lex's family descend upon me." She stormed into the room and dropped into a padded chair next to him. "I'm not even dressed."

"Here are some things I picked up for you. I had to guess at the sizes though."

Jane grabbed the bag and dropped it on the floor without even glancing at it. She was annoyed with him, but was grateful to have something to wear that didn't leave her butt open to the world.

"Why didn't you wake me up or at least warn me?"

"I tried, but you were dead to the world. I didn't realize Mrs. D'Angelo would get here quite so fast. They didn't even stop in the waiting area and call the desk like you're supposed to. I've been here all night so I could keep an eye on who was coming and going but they took me by surprise. They blew right past me and stormed the nurses station."

He actually appeared embarrassed—and a little afraid.

Good.

She took the bag of clothes—Wal-Mart again—and opened

it without a word. Let him sweat for a bit.

Mac obviously didn't have experience buying women's clothing. Jane found a gray sweat suit, a gray sports bra, a three-pack of white T-shirts, a three-pack of white granny underwear, a package of athletic socks, and a pair of white canvas tennis shoes. At this point Jane didn't care if she was dressed in couture or not, she just wanted to be covered.

"Sheila, one of the nurses, said you could use the shower down the hall when you woke up. There's a toothbrush and some toiletries in the other bag over there."

Jane could guess which nurse was Sheila. The bag had tiny sample sizes of shampoo, conditioner, soap, toothpaste and body lotion. She'd have to make sure to thank Sheila the next time she saw her. A shower would do wonders to improve her morale.

"I think I will take that shower. Don't disappear on me. I want to talk to you." Jane gave him a stern look and picked up the bags. She wasn't facing Lex's family again without reinforcements. When she went back in, she wanted someone with a gun.

Chapter Twenty

Clean, dry and dressed in an over-large sweat suit, Jane felt almost ready to face the combined wrath of the D'Angelo clan. Okay, she'd rather face one of Susie's goons dressed in nothing but plastic wrap, but she felt better than she had before.

Mac waited for her in the family lounge and they walked through the double doors to the CCU together. Her tennis shoes squeaked on the tile floor, but she could barely hear the noise over the shouts coming from Lex's room.

Security waited by the nurses' station and they kept casting threatening looks down the hall. Mac winced at a particularly loud spate of Italian. Wonderful. A former FBI agent was afraid of a group of women half his size.

My hero.

"Ma! Lay off, and quiet down before they throw you out," Lex's voice rang above the din.

He was awake. Jane practically ran the rest of the way to the room.

"Jane. It's about time. Where the hell have you been?"

He sat up in bed and several of the tubes had been removed in her absence. Someone had shaved him, given him a sponge bath and combed his hair. Jane's heart took another slow roll in her chest as he held out his hand to her.

"Well good morning to you too." A smile pulled at the corners of her mouth. It was so good to see him sitting up and clear headed.

"Come on, make some room for her. Theresa, why don't you ask the nurse to take this catheter out of me? And, Sophia, can you find out when I can get the hell out of this place?"

The two youngest D'Angelo's looked to their mother for permission before leaving to do Lex's bidding. They both shot Mac and Jane curious glances as they left the room.

"Momma, this is Jane Farmer. Dr. Jane Farmer, and my boss, Steve McLean." He reached for Jane's hand and grabbed it as soon as she got close enough. "It's because of the two of them that I'm alive."

"All the credit belongs to Jane," Mac said. "She got you to safety and alerted us to the possibility of further danger." He didn't mention Susie's name or anything about the mission.

Jane took the hint and made a mental note to keep the information to herself as well.

"My family and I thank you for saving Luther's life. I apologize for speaking to you like I did when I first saw you. I was a little scared."

Her accent was barely noticeable now and Jane saw warmth fill her eyes as she gazed at her son.

"That's perfectly understandable. You had just heard your son had been shot and there I was posing as his wife. It would get anyone upset," Jane soothed, using her best therapist voice.

She couldn't believe the difference in Mrs. D'Angelo. Talk about rapid mood shifts. Barely an hour ago the woman had been ready to ride Jane out of town, now she was apologizing and looking at their joined hands with affection. She'd seen more emotion in Lex's mom in one hour than she'd seen in her mother in thirty years.

"You're a nice girl." She patted Jane's cheek with work-roughened hands. "Where are you from?"

"Connecticut, ma'am."

"What about your family?"

"Ma!" Lex seemed almost horrified at his mother's interrogation. "Do you think I can have a few minutes alone with my boss and partner? There are some things we have to clear up. Work stuff."

Mrs. D'Angelo's eyes narrowed and she gave her son an assessing glare. After she fawned over him a bit, she leaned over and kissed him on both cheeks before whispering something in Italian.

Lex glanced quickly at Jane and answered back in Italian. The sound of his voice spilling those rounded syllables sent a burst of heat through Jane's system. What would it be like to hear him whisper love words to her in his mother's native language?

A blush filled her cheeks and she shifted her feet nervously. She really shouldn't be thinking about sex with Lex when his mother was right next to her.

"You'll come to dinner when Luther gets out of the hospital? I'll make manicotti. You need a good meal." She kissed both of Jane's cheeks too and gestured to her daughters to follow her out.

Jane looked at Lex, bewildered. "What was that all about?"

"I told you my mother would want to feed you. Anyone who doesn't have hips the size of a Chevy, she wants to fatten up. Don't worry about it." He pulled her closer to him and kissed her knuckles.

The feel of his lips on her hand sent tingles all the way down to her toes. He obviously felt better today.

Mac cleared his throat behind them and Jane's head snapped around. She'd forgotten he was still in the room.

"Now that I have you both here and not under sedation, I'd like to hear the whole story."

Jane sat in the chair next to the bed and let Lex handle things while her mind spun. He wasn't acting like she'd expected and she needed a minute to sort it out.

She didn't know what she thought would happen when everything was over. Maybe he'd shake her hand and move on or give her a lame one-liner like "I'll call you sometime."

In her mind she was the one who was going to have to convince him to continue their relationship. During her shower she'd practiced arguments until she could counter anything he threw at her.

She wasn't prepared for him to want to have her around. He couldn't really want to continue their relationship, could he?

Lex's voice broke into her frantic thoughts. "I couldn't have done it without Jane's help. She played Jim Bob like a pro. And it was her quick thinking that got us out of the lab too."

"I really didn't do much. Honestly, I thought James Robert was behind the whole thing until Susie caught us in the office." Jane's stomach bottomed out as she remembered seeing Susie holding the gun on them. "I was mostly window dressing."

"Bull."

"I agree with Lex. You were an integral part of the success of this mission. It's never easy to act without backup or resources. The two of you managed to not only bust open a national drug ring, but also discover the mole at EIS. For which

I'm especially grateful."

Mac didn't say it, but Jane could tell the idea of a traitor in his midst had bothered him a great deal.

"Hey, what happened with Alice anyway?" Lex asked.

"After Jane confirmed my suspicions, I pulled her hard drive and called the police. They found her at the airport, waiting for a flight to Aruba."

"Susie must have called before getting nabbed by the police," Jane said.

"What's going to happen now?"

"I'm not sure yet. The DA is going to have to figure out what's a criminal charge and what's civil. Technically, telling her friend about Sarah wasn't illegal."

"But using EIS resources to locate DEA patrols sure as hell was!" Lex growled. His hand tightened on Jane's slightly battered one and she winced.

"I know. Like I said, I'm going to have to go over things with the DA to make sure all the charges are accurate and stick. I'm also going to have to do a complete overhaul of the computer system to find out how she accessed those files. It's encrypted information and she shouldn't have been able to get into it."

"Crap," Lex groaned. "That means everything is going to be down for months."

Jane glared at him. "What are you worried about? You're not going anywhere for a while with that bullet hole in your side."

Did he want to go on another assignment so soon?

"I know, but when we're not on assignment we get stuck doing paperwork. You have no idea how much paperwork is involved in billing and filing reports and we won't have Alice to help out. I hate filing."

An idea popped into Jane's head and out of her mouth before she had a chance to stop it. "I could help. Filing is one of my specialties, and I know more about billing than I ever wanted to from when I had my own practice. At least with you I wouldn't have to deal with insurance agencies."

"We can't ask you to do that. You're a doctor, not a secretary," Mac said.

"I'm also currently unemployed. I could help out around the agency until I find another job or you find a replacement for Alice," Jane said, liking the idea. She'd be doing something constructive while she figured out what direction her life was headed in and she'd be able to be near Lex. It was a win-win situation as far as she was concerned.

"Listen to her, Mac. You know you can trust her and she doesn't mind filing. Quick. Hire her before she comes to her senses!"

"I had a something else in mind for a woman of Dr. Farmer's talents."

"Oh?" Jane asked. He'd said something about her working as support before but she'd been rather confused and didn't remember it very well.

"What are you talking about? I don't want to see Jane hurt. She's taken enough bruising for EIS already."

"Something more behind the scenes."

Lex opened his mouth to protest but Jane cut him off. "Shh. I want to hear what he has to say."

"Are you kidding me? You almost got shot back at the ministry. How can you think about putting yourself at risk again?" He shouted, then clutched his side in pain.

"It's my decision to make. I might refuse, but it will be my decision." She stared right into his flaming eyes and dared him to argue with her.

He didn't look happy but he kept his mouth closed.

Turning to Mac she asked, "Now, what is it you had in mind?"

"Profiling. With your background and instincts you could work up a psychiatric profile on potential targets for our field agents. Your input could be invaluable."

"I'm not a profiler, I'm a therapist. I don't have the training or expertise to do that job."

"EIS could provide any additional training necessary. You have good instincts about people, that's worth more than any schooling. I think you'd be a great fit for EIS. Besides profiling you could help prepare agents before they go undercover. With your knowledge of human behavior, you could give them some great tips about how, say an abused child would react to his abuser."

Jane didn't answer right away. Her first impulse was to laugh at him and tell him he was nuts. She counseled people, she didn't profile them. But the more he spoke, the more sense he made.

"What if I'm wrong? What if I evaluate someone and I'm completely off the mark? Psychology isn't an exact science."

"That happens to all agents. People make mistakes. Your evaluation would just be one of the tools used, not the end all of the case."

"You're not seriously considering this, are you?" Lex asked. "You're a talk-show host for God's sake."

"I was a talk-show host. I got fired." His concern was obvious, but she couldn't let his feelings run her life. "I'm not going to make any decisions right now. I need a little time to get re-oriented. But I am thinking about it. I'm sorry if that upsets you, but I can't back down just to make you happy."

"I'm just worried about you, babe. You almost got killed."

"So did you," she said softly. Her bones had melted into mush at the emotion in his eyes.

"Yeah, but I'm trained for this stuff. You're not."

"She could be," Mac said from the end of the bed.

"You keep out of this. All you see is the advantage she'd be to the company, not the danger she'd be in. Someone has to watch out for her safety."

"I can see to my own safety. I know what I want out of life, and it isn't hiding away anymore."

"I'll leave you two to discuss this." Mac backed out of the room.

Lex waited until Mac left before rounding on Jane.

"Do you know what you're in for if you sign on with him? He's only shown you his suave businessman face. You've never seen him tear a strip off someone when he's pissed off. He can be damn ruthless."

"I'm sure he can. I've also seen him scared to death about you. Don't tell me that he purposely puts his employees into danger."

He grunted. "No, he does his best to minimize the risks."

Jane brought Lex's hand up to rub across her cheek. "I know you don't want to see me hurt. I don't want to see you in danger either, but we—"

"Hold it right there—" he cut her off, "—I know what you're about to say. We didn't make any commitments. It was due to the dangerous circumstances and all that other crap. Well that's bullshit. You're not the type of woman to go to bed with someone you don't care about. You can't tell me that we don't have something between us whether we talked about it or not.

You're mine. Got it?"

Jane's mouth dropped open at his diatribe. She should really be insulted at his macho speech but she was too thrilled to be angry. He didn't want it to be over either.

Still, she couldn't let him get away with his caveman tactics. If she let him do that once, he'd walk all over her for the rest of her life.

"Do I get a say in this?"

"No." He set his mouth stubbornly. "Fine! What do you have to say about it? And don't try any of that psychoanalysis crap about how intense situations create insubstantial emotions. I've been through plenty of intense situations and I've never felt like this before."

More warm tingles bubbled through her veins like champagne.

"All I was going to say was that even though I don't want to see you hurt, I can't expect you to live in a box for the rest of your life. If we want to live life to the fullest we have to take a few risks. I'm sure I'll be scared to death every time you leave on a mission, but if I'm working for EIS I can do my darndest to make sure you have all the support you need to come back to me safely."

"You're not going to argue about the 'you're mine' comment?"

"How can I argue about the truth? Everything you said so indelicately is true. But you forgot one thing. It works both ways. You're mine too."

"You got that right."

He pulled her down for a kiss that curled her toes. His mouth took possession of hers as if he'd never let her go. That was just fine with Jane. She didn't want to be anywhere else.

The sound of applause broke them apart and Jane jerked to attention. Lex's family and half the nursing staff stood outside the curtained doorway clapping madly. Mrs. D'Angelo dabbed at the corners of her eyes and his sisters laughed through their tears.

"Welcome to the family," Lex said wryly.

"You must come stay with us until Luther is out of the hospital. We'll take care of you too."

"And you thought working for EIS was going to be risky?" Lex murmured.

Jane gazed at Lex's battered form and then at his family's smiling faces. The risks were definitely worth it. Sometimes you had to take a leap of faith. At least Lex would be there to catch her.

About the Author

To learn more about Arianna Hart, please visit www.ariannahart.com. Send an email to Arianna at ari@ariannahart.com or join her Yahoo! group to join in the fun with other readers as well as Arianna Hart. friendsofari-subscribe@yahoogroups.com

All small towns have secrets. This one could be deadly.

The Seduction of Shamus O'Rourke
© *2007 N.J. Walters*
Book 4 of Jamesville.

After her father's death, Cyndi Marks returns to Jamesville, determined to settle here and lay the ghosts of years ago to rest once and for all. But the past has a way of catching up—and hanging on.

When her car breaks down outside of town, a handsome stranger stops to help. He intrigues and attracts her, but then she discovers who he is.

Shamus O'Rourke enjoys his job, his family and small town living. What he's missing is someone with whom to share it. Immediately drawn to Cyndi, he is determined to get closer to her, even as he senses her pulling away.

But not everyone in Jamesville is happy to see Cyndi. People are hiding secrets. Secrets they would kill to protect. When violence erupts in her home, Cyndi turns to the only person in town she can trust—Shamus.

In a situation where family loyalties are strained, Cyndi's life is threatened and everyone is a suspect, will their emerging love survive?

Available now in ebook and print from Samhain Publishing.

Enjoy the following excerpt from

The Seduction of Shamus O'Rourke...

Jamesville, Maine. It looked so peaceful nestled down in the valley below, but Cyndi knew that even a small town had dirty little secrets. Turning her back on the picturesque scene, she strode to the trunk of her car. She needed to keep focused on the task at hand and right now that included getting her car back on the road so she could reach her destination before dark.

The sun was low in the afternoon sky, but she had an hour or so until it finally sank. Lots of time to change a flat tire and get to the lawyer's office before it closed for the day. Unlocking her trunk, she pocketed her keys and hauled out her two suitcases, setting them beside the car. Next came her laptop, which she tucked into the backseat for safekeeping. Two boxes containing her pillows and comforter, specialty teas, and her favorite snacks were next. She figured she'd need all the comforts she could get. She was under no illusion that the task ahead of her would be easy.

Cyndi ignored the small voice in the back of her head that whispered she didn't have to stay. She'd made her decision and she wasn't about to back down now. It was time for her to face down the demons of her past and put them to rest once and for all. The only way to do that was to settle in Jamesville. She'd put all her belongings in storage, let the lease on her apartment lapse, and quit her job as manager of an upscale bed and breakfast. For better or worse, she was here to stay.

Dragging out the jack and the spare tire, she carried them one at a time to the front of the car. The left-hand tire was as flat as a pancake. She must have picked up a nail or something. As soon as she hit town, she'd have to go to a garage and get it seen to.

As she was shoving the jack beneath the car, she heard another vehicle rumbling up behind her. She scooted in front of her car, not wanting to be out in the road as the other vehicle passed. She'd pulled her car as far off the road as she could, but the shoulder wasn't that wide and part of the vehicle was still on the pavement. A dusty, blue truck passed her, but the brake lights flashed almost immediately, and the vehicle rolled to a stop several yards up the road.

Cyndi climbed back into the driver's seat and locked all the doors. Maybe she was overreacting, but a woman on her own, on a fairly deserted stretch of road, couldn't be too careful. She knew what Jamesville used to be like, but that was a long time ago. The whole world seemed to have changed in the intervening years.

The truck door opened and a long, jean-clad leg came into view, quickly followed by another. The man who got out of the vehicle was huge, standing at least several inches over six feet. His shoulders were wide, straining the seams of his dirty, white T-shirt. The short sleeves of the shirt did nothing to hide his thick biceps and muscular forearms. His jeans were faded white at the knees and crotch area. Cyndi forced herself to look away. A stranger was coming toward her, and she was staring at his crotch. It had to be the stress she'd been under making her so loopy. Still, she did enjoy the view.

His large, booted feet quickly ate up the distance between them. Cyndi reached into her purse and yanked out her phone, ready to call for help if necessary.

The man stopped beside her door, leaned down and tapped on the window. "Didn't mean to frighten you, ma'am."

Cyndi got her first, really good look at his face and it

started her heart pounding, but not from fear. The man was gorgeous, in a rough sort of way. His thick, molasses-brown hair was tied back at the nape, falling just below his shoulders. His face was all sharp angles and planes; his nose was large, but somehow suited his face. Eyebrows the same color as his hair were straight slashes above a pair of concerned, blue-gray eyes, eyes the same color as the sky just before a storm.

"Ma'am?" She heard his voice through the glass and realized she was sitting there like a fool simply staring at him.

Quickly she rolled the window down, but just a crack. "I'm sorry. What did you say?"

He tilted his head to one side, staring at her. Cyndi knew she looked a mess. She'd been traveling for hours, and the past few weeks had been extremely stressful. She knew she had dark circles under her eyes and wasn't wearing any makeup, save her clear lip balm. Her days of dressing to please other people were long over.

"I said that I didn't mean to frighten you." He smiled then, a slight upturn of the corners of his mouth, but the effect was devastating.

Butterflies danced in her stomach and she felt a throbbing between her thighs. She shook her head, desperately trying to fight the unwanted burst of physical attraction. She was thirty-nine years old, for heaven's sake, long past the stage of being ruled by her hormones. And he looked to be at least ten years younger than her.

"A woman alone can't be too careful these days." His words echoed her earlier thoughts. "You stay put in the car and I'll take care of that flat tire for you."

"No," she snapped. Realizing what she'd done, she softened her tone. After all, it wasn't his fault she was attracted to him. All he'd done was stop and offer to help. "That's fine. I'll take care of it myself."

He scrubbed his hand across his jaw and her eyes followed the action. She could see the five o'clock shadow on his chin. It made him appear even sexier, if that was possible. There was something elemental about this man. Even dressed in old work boots, faded jeans and a dirty T-shirt, there was an air of barely restrained power about him.

"I figured you could handle the problem on your own, ma'am, but there's no need for that now that I'm here."

Was he for real?

GREAT
CHEAP
FUN

Discover eBooks!

THE FASTEST WAY TO GET THE HOTTEST NAMES

Get your favorite authors on your favorite reader, long before they're
out in print! Ebooks from Samhain go wherever you go, and work with
whatever you carry—Palm, PDF, Mobi, and more.

Printed in the United States
136364LV00001B/169/P